The Miracle of Stalag 8A
Beauty Beyond the Horror:

Olivier Messiaen
and the
Quartet for the End of Time

Bird Brain Publishing

Bird Brain Publishing

The Miracle of Stalag 8A
Beauty Beyond the Horror:

Olivier Messiaen
and the
Quatour pour la Fin du Temps
"Quartet for the End of Time"

by

John William McMullen
© 2010

Bird Brain Publishing
Evansville, Indiana

Graphic cover design by Whitney Arvin.
Contributing Editor: Katie Meyer.

Bird Brain Publishing is an imprint of Bird Brain Productions.

www.birdbrainproductions.com

McMullen, John William
  The Miracle of Stalag 8A / by John William McMullen
  Summary: French composer Olivier Messiaen is drafted into the French Army at the beginning of World War II and after being captured by Nazis he composes his work the Quartet for the End of Time while imprisoned at Stalag 8A.

ISBN 13: 978-0-9826255-2-1   Paperback
ISBN 13: 978-0-9826255-3-8   Hardback

  Printed in the United States of America

M229m

To

Columba Kelly, O.S.B.

In homage to the Angel of the Apocalypse, who raises a hand towards Heaven saying, 'There shall be no more Time'.

- Olivier Messiaen's inscription on the title page of *Quatour pour la Fin du Temps*

"On 15 January 1941, in a German prison camp in Silesia, music triumphed over Time, breaking free of rhythm and liberating a quartet of French prisoners and their listeners from the horrors of their time. The Quartet for the End of Time has earned its place in the canon and history of Western music, but, more important, it has earned its place in our hearts. Its musical beauty, at once terrifying and sublime, exalts listeners and performers alike, and the story of its creators stands as a testament to the powers of music and human will to transcend the most terrible of times."

– Rebecca Rischin, Associate Professor, Ohio University School of Music, and author of FOR THE END OF TIME: THE STORY OF THE MESSIAEN QUARTET (Cornell University Press, 2003; 2006).

Olivier Messiaen

"I suffer from an unknown, distant music."

– From *L'Ame en bourgeon* (The Burgeoning Soul),
a book of poems written for Olivier Messiaen
by his mother, Cécile Sauvage, before he was born.

Prologue

War

May 1940

Klaxon air-raid horns sounded forth as the shrill whine of German bombers approached; the lightning-like flash and rumble of dropping bombs approached like a swift moving monstrous thunderstorm. The German planes filled the sky like a murder of crows; the screaming Stuka bombers dove to the treetops, strafed with machine gun fire, and bombed the French troops and French countryside. The howling madness and exploding ammunition was deafening as flame and smoke and a hail of rock and mud enveloped Olivier Messiaen and his companions.

Messiaen's uniform stank of mud and blood as it clung to his sweaty, gangly figure. The thick lenses of his horn-rimmed glasses crookedly framed his round face; the lenses were scratched and frames bent from all the military maneuvers.

He found himself tangled in a forest floor; the sweet smell of lilac and roses a dichotomy to the gouging pain of briars and thorns in his arms and legs as he sought cover amid the flash of machine gun-fire and random explosions. He trembled as his haversack was covered in debris. In the intermittent flashes of light, he opened the sack, thumbed through his photographs of his wife, Claire, and two-year-old son, Pascal, secured the pages of his musical notes, and caressed the cover of his Bible and prayed for courage. The strafing, explosions and sights and smell of death surrounded him. With the onslaught of war Messiaen held tightly to his collection of musical compositions. He feared more for the loss of his music than the loss of his life.

O God, deliver me from evil.

Before the war his life was well ordered. He ardently longed to be with Claire and Pascal, composing and teaching music, and playing the church organ as before.

Now he was praying for deliverance from German bombs. If he ever made it home alive, would his music be recognized?

Another series of Stuka bombers bore down on the woods and strafed with machine gun fire while larger planes followed dropping bombs. He scrambled for cover, crawling to safety. As he hunkered down, the clashing chords of the whining sounds of the Stuka sirens, air raid horns, and whistling bombs evoked a musical memory.

"(The composer) Paul Dukas
always told me to listen to the birds."

- Olivier Messiaen

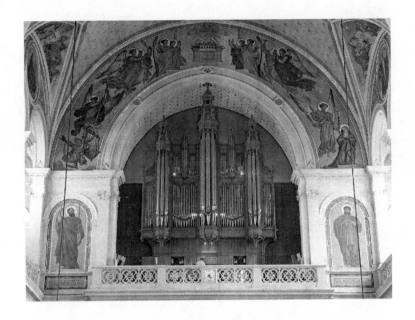

The organ at *Sainte-Trinité* Church in Paris
where Olivier Messiaen served as organist.

Chapter 1

The Eve of War

3 September 1939

Olivier Messiaen was composing at his summer Alpine retreat at Petichet south of Grenoble; the home looked across Lac de Laffrey and beyond to the snowy vista of Grand Serre. The summer months were the most conducive to composing for Olivier, given his teaching commitments at the *Ecole Normale de Musique* and duties at *La Église de la Sainte-Trinité* (the Church of the Holy Trinity) in Paris during the year. At a distance of nearly 600 kilometers from Paris, Petichet in the Daufiné Province afforded him the peace and distance he needed to fulfill his life's vocation and work.

Under his black beret, the round faced, tall, wiry 31 year old pressed his horn-rimmed glasses up the bridge of his nose. In his comfortable tailored grey slacks, neatly starched long sleeve dress shirt with gold cuff links, Olivier Messiaen sat on the porch listening to the chorus of birds. The song thrush, several warblers, the blackcap songbird, the nightingale imitating every birdcall and song he heard, and the husky cry of the raven, among other birds, filled the morning air with their voices.

Messiaen gazed at the lush green valley below and the deep blue of Lake Laffrey, making notations of the differing birdsongs as well as working out a musical idea on his ever-present notepad. His morning meditation and appreciation of birdsong was an act of faith.

Since childhood, Messiaen had been irresistibly drawn to music. He was reading music in his head as a young child and he knew early on that he was a musician. His mother had penned *L'Ame en bourgeon* (The Burgeoning Soul), a book of poems for him before he was born. One of the lines read: *I suffer from an unknown, distant music.* Messiaen had always pondered the book of poems as somehow prophetic. His mother had been dead now for twelve years, yet grief remained.

This avant-garde composer who was a leader among the new musicians of Paris had one major flaw among the haute: he was a devout Roman Catholic. He knew his music was misunderstood; a mystery both pondered and ridiculed. He intended for his music to lead people to an experience of the divine.

Glancing away from a couple of bantering ravens, he eyed an approaching figure. He was expecting no one. In time Messiaen recognized the man by his uniform. This could only mean one thing.

"Monsieur Olivier Messiaen?" the young soldier asked, tipping his hat.

"I am Messiaen." He stood, adjusting his sleeves and fumbling with the cufflink of his left arm. Olivier's age made him eligible to be called up for military service.

"I have a letter of dispatch from military headquarters. Sir, you are to report to the central Paris railway station within 48 hours for military duty."

"Forty-eight hours? I'm on holiday." He shifted his weight from one leg to the other, turning towards the house.

"Haven't you heard?" the soldier asked.

Messiaen's eyes met the young soldiers'.

"I'm sorry, Sir. The Germans invaded Poland two days ago and France and Britain have declared war on Germany today."

"Hitler," Messiaen murmured. "War has finally come."

"I'm afraid so, Sir."

Messiaen's eyes darted to the house again. His wife, Claire, was visible in the porch window; her face spoke concern.

Claire seemed wispy, at times frail and feeble, even physically beyond her years, not the vivacious young composer and violinist Claire Delbos he had married in 1932. He was anxious for her state of mind. After her miscarriages and especially since becoming a mother, she had changed. She tried to maintain a smile and cheerful spirit, but her eyes and posture betrayed her. In the two years since Pascal's birth, the light in her eyes had dimmed and her thoughts were often unclear. Once the light in his life, now her candle was flickering, and he feared her light was being extinguished just as his own mother's light had gone out much too early. It seemed Claire was a bird who was forgetting how to sing, whose feeble wings forbade it from flight.

Messiaen hesitated to go in the house as his feet stumbled on the rug. His stomach moiled as he slumped back down in his wicker chair. Claire opened the door and Messiaen struggled to stand, his legs unwilling.

"Well?" Claire's eyes were unblinking as she held their two-year-old son, Pascal, in her arms, balancing him on her left hip. "What did that soldier want?"

"France and England have declared war on Germany."

Claire's hazel eyes glistened as her face fell. She reached for Olivier and he held her and Pascal close as she began to cry.

"You cannot return to Paris," Olivier explained. "If the Germans break through the Maginot line, they will certainly make for the city."

"Then where can we go?" Claire asked, her words lost to tears as she buried her face in Messiaen's chest.

"You will be safe with your mother at your family's château in the Cantal Mountains."

Claire's eyes and demeanor seemed vacant of all hope. Messiaen knew she had suffered melancholia after the birth of Pascal, but he worried what their separation would do to her health.

Messiaen quickly made plans to evacuate her and Pascal from Petichet to Neussargues to be with her mother and sister at the Delbos's Château St. Benoît in the Cantal Mountains of the Auvergne Province of France, nearly 420 kilometers south of Paris, and hopefully far enough from any advancing German troops.

She held him close in her arms.

During the First World War, Olivier Messiaen's own father, Pierre Messiaen, had been called up to serve the country in the war against Germany. Olivier Messiaen was seven when his father left and he didn't see him again for nearly four years. Now he would not be able to shield Pascal from war just as his own father could not. He had a fleeting memory of his father in uniform.

Now Messiaen's duty to his family and the Church would be replaced with his duty to country and his fellow soldiers. The similarities between his father's life and his own call to service seemed eerily preternatural.

The next day was cool with sun and clouds as Messiaen saw Claire and Pascal off at the train station. Claire was struggling with her own pain and seemed overwhelmed with the demands of their two-year-old son. Messiaen's consolation was that she would be with her mother and her sister.

Olivier and Claire embraced on the Petichet station's platform and wept as they kissed as if for the last time; he nestled Pascal close.

"I will write you, my love," Claire said, behind her tears as she stepped onto the passenger coach with Pascal in her arms.

"And I you," Olivier promised as the train jerked forward in a burst of steam while the engineer blew the final whistle announcing the train's departure. A whirlwind of loose papers and dust traced through the air in the wake of the train.

Messiaen watched the train move westward en route to Neussargues, hopefully safe from any German aggression. The voice of the locomotive cried out as a flutter of sparrows twittered and flew through the mist of coal cinders and smoke. Messiaen stood on the platform until the train was completely out of sight.

*****

When Messiaen returned to Paris, he was anxious about his deployment to the German Front and made his way to *La Église de la Sainte-Trinité* where he was titular organist. Messiaen was deep in meditation as he engaged the organ's keys and lost himself in the sonorous chords. He was perfecting his newest work, *Les corps glorieux*, (the glorious bodies), and engaged in the section *Combat de la mort et de la vie* (Combat of death and of life).

Rumors of Hitler and his intentions for war had echoed through Europe for several years, but now they were no longer rumors. The declaration of war would now separate him from his wife and son and would take him away from composing and serving as the church organist at *Sainte-Trinité* as well as his teaching post at *Ecole de Musique.*

As he sought to work out his personal dilemma through the pipes, the older parishioners would likely lament that the devil was working his way through those same pipes.

Messiaen's thoughts were on his own personal struggle between life and death, chaos and order. His desire to compose and be with his wife and son were now lost in the chaotic sounds of the pipes as his hands and feet punctuated notes and chords.

He could scarcely take it all in, knowing that his son Pascal would be bereft of explanation or understanding of what was happening and why. His emptiness and confusion blasted out of the organ's pipes and echoed off the stone and marble of the church.

During the Great War, Messiaen's uncles Leon and Paul had died in battle and he feared his own father would soon follow. In 1916, Messiaen's piano teacher, Marcel Dupré, took him to the organ loft of Saint Sulpice in Paris and allowed Messiaen to experiment with the instrument. The nine-year-old Messiaen discovered that the pipe organ was loud enough and big enough to express his deepest grief and anger at his father's absence. The emotional chaos of loss against the order of Bach and Widor congealed with the sounds of Ravel and Dukas, yielding clashing chords of dissonance, erupting at his fingertips.

His thoughts were interrupted when a breathless Marcel Dupré climbed the stairs distracting Messiaen from his work of prayer.

"*Mon Dieu*, Olivier!" Dupré called out to him from the steps to the organ where Olivier was seated. "One of your students rang me and told me you were back in Paris." Dupré was organist at *Saint-Sulpice* in Paris.

The discord of the pipes echoed into silence. Dupré's gentle face, aquiline nose, and penetrating eyes were a welcome sight for Messiaen.

"*Oui*. I have been recalled compliments of *der Führer*. I am being deployed today. I came by the church to pick up a few pieces of music to keep my mind occupied."

"What are you practicing?" he asked.

"My latest work, *Les corps glorieux.* I finished the first draft last week at Petichet."

"I hear great conflict in the pipes."

"I have always preferred that which frightens." Messiaen tried to put the impending war with Germany out of his mind. "But there is always a crucifix that points the way to glory. The human heart is an abyss which can only be filled by the divine."

Dupré said nothing; Messiaen was good at uttering the enigmatic and mysterious.

An emergency vehicle's siren shattered the silence between them.

"There's fear in the streets," Dupré said.

"Yes, I am sure of it," Messiaen looked down, closed his eyes, and sighed as he pushed in the open stops of the organ.

There had been fear in the Parisians for some time: the uncertainty of the economic depression, hunger, government in crisis, and political upheaval. Now war has come a second time in little more than 20 years. For many of the older generations of French, this would be the third war in 70 years counting the Franco-Prussian War of 1870-71 and the Great War from 1914-18.

"Olivier, you can't be serious about leaving Paris," Dupré regained his attention. "Certainly there is a civilian detail that can accommodate you. Your eyesight is poor and your health is fragile. Your frame is that of an artist, not a soldier!"

"I am to board the train for Metz this afternoon." Messiaen rested his fingers on the organ keys and closed his eyes.

Dupré glanced at his wristwatch and explained that he had to get back to the conservatoire.

Messiaen looked up, promptly collected his music from the organ, placed it in his satchel, closed the instrument's lid over the keys, and descended the narrow stairwell behind Dupré.

Messiaen returned to his home at the Villa du Danube located on the Right Bank of the River Seine. As he opened the door, the absence of his wife and son was palpable. His night alone in the house was restless.

The next morning Messiaen set aside his civilian clothes and donned the French army uniform. The olive-colored suit sagged on his lanky figure. It was a poor fit for the natty composer. He then wandered through the house, mindlessly viewing a few paintings and observing his and Claire's possessions, all the while his thoughts on the prospect of his dying in the war. He then began to purposely grab some necessities before making one last tour of the house looking for a few scattered items to place in his haversack: musical compositions, his bible, a few photographs, and a handful of other personal items.

As he prepared to leave, the piano in the corner of the front room beckoned his attention. He reverently walked over to it and ran his fingers along the keys, spending time reflecting upon the hours, days, and months he had spent before the instrument composing and playing. His eyes moved from the keys to the family portrait that hung on the wall above. He studied the faces of Claire and Pascal vowing to never forget them.

He turned, picked up his valise and haversack, and locked the door behind him. As he shut the door, he lowered his eyes and prayed for his wife and son. *This may well be the last time I will ever see Paris.* The thought vanished from his conscious mind as quickly as it had emerged.

As a result of the declaration of war, everything he knew was being taken from him: his wife and son, time for composing and performing, and time with God, playing the organ in Church.

*****

Rain clouds covered Paris as a chilly September air blew. Messiaen mulled over the reality of war as he made his way to the train station. At the end of the Great War or World War I, even though Germany had been made to bear the burden of the war and all its destruction, France herself was in political and economic upheaval. Now, with Germany on the move, France was in great disarray. The left had embraced isolationism while the right seemed willing to accommodate dictatorship. Only the French Communists vocally opposed the rise of Nazism.

Despite Hitler's rhetoric of anti-Semitism and the violence of *Kristallnacht*, many French did not openly condemn Germany. Even though *Kristallnacht* had revealed the true face of Nazism to the world, the threat of the Third Reich was still disregarded by many. Many of the French either ignored Hitler or considered war only a remote possibility, and were in no mood to go on the offense. Many Parisians believed Paris would always be free. They dreaded war and the fate of another war with Germany weighed upon the French heart. Though war had been declared, certainly diplomacy would avert the disaster of war this time. Certainly.

Messiaen's own thoughts were on his son Pascal. Would Pascal, not quite two years of age, be without his father for four years? *What if I cannot watch or see my son grow up! What a terrible sorrow. Or what if I am killed as were my Uncles Leon and Paul? God forbid. O Lord, intervene and prevent the madness of war from ravaging France once again.*

The memory of the melody of Maurice Ravel's piano work *Gaspard de la Nuit* (Gaspard of the Night) distracted him from his quandary. The piece was one of his favorites as a child. What jewel-like, dark, mysterious musical treasures had Gaspard bestowed upon Messiaen via Maurice Ravel? As Messiaen made his way toward the Maginot Line he knew that beyond No Man's Land was the Siegfried line. Would the Germans attack?

Approaching the depot under a gloomy sky, morose thoughts occupied Messiaen's mind once again as he caught sight of a large peregrine falcon ominously perched atop the building. The air was charged with the sounds of wheels clacking on the tracks, metal scraping against metal, rails shrilly singing and the crackle and hiss of the electric trains with their tooting whistles.

The station was dark and desolate, in ill repair with peeling paint; the smell of the sewer rancid; the tracks were littered with broken and shattered wine bottles; and cigar and cigarette butts dappled the passenger platform. Trash and paper tumbled in the wind as early autumn leaves hovered and landed in a dance between life and death.

Messiaen read and reread the musical scores as if he had to hurriedly etch them in his memory; likewise he did the same with the photographs of his wife and son and his deceased mother.

It began to rain, heaven's cold sorrow at the spectacle of war.

Soon he heard the grinding hiss of the locomotive, its clanging bell, whining whistle, and clanking of wheels and rails, heralding its arrival into the station. The cacophony of the sounds of the impending war and the lonely moan of the locomotive hauling soldiers off to war grieved his heart and pierced his soul, filling his mind with thoughts of death and life and their titanic struggle.

He had made this journey before, but never like this before.

"Every bird is a living leitmotif.
The song of the meadowlark is extremely jubilant
and alleluia-like.
The wood thrush's song is full of sunlight,
almost sacramental.
The song of the virtuoso warbler is
Debussy rewritten by Stockhausen."

– Olivier Messiaen

Chapter 2

The Phoney War

Established at Metz, Messiaen wrote Claire often.

1 November 1939

> *Mon Chérie Claire,*
>
> *At the moment I am doing a rather gentler kind of soldiering: I am giving harmony lessons to fellow soldiers.*
>
> *I attended the Holy Day Mass today of All Saints. I played the pipe organ for the soldiers. Some of the men haven't been to church since their youth. Our chaplain heard confessions and said Mass.*
>
> *How are you, my beloved Mi? And our son Pascal? Tell him I pray for him daily, and for his sweet mother.*
>
> *No sign of German activity yet. I suppose the newspapers are right. This does seem to be a phoney war. Yet I fear that the Germans are up to no good.*
>
> *After all the hard work associated with the infantry, it is hard for me to think about music, to return to it as to a comforting elder sister. However, every night, during the hours which are meant to be for sleeping, I resolve to read a few pages of the pocket scores which are arranged with loving care at the bottom of my haversack. Whenever I am able to find a light, I read them closely, analyzing forms, harmonies, and timbres in symphonies by Beethoven, or other works by Ravel, Stravinsky, or Debussy.*

My love, Oli

*****

Olivier Messiaen's unit had now been encamped at Metz, working along the Maginot Line, for over two months. All of the men knew that this area of Lorraine had been the battlefield between the French and Germans for hundreds of years. Ever in their minds were the ghosts of the "*Zone Rouge,*" the "Red Zone," of the 1916 Battle of Verdun, or *Meuse Mill*, where over 60,000 French soldiers died, 100,000 went missing, and over 200,000 were wounded or maimed. Though that battle of total war had occurred over 20 years before, hundreds of square miles of the marred hills of the battlefield were still pockmarked with craters from the untold millions of shells and grenades. It remained the final resting place of many of the dead and missing.

None of the men wanted to repeat their fathers' war.

Messiaen's olive khaki uniform and cloak hung on his gangly figure, quite a contrast to his preferred dress and appearance. He looked out of place in the military with his horn-rimmed glasses and their thick lenses; his eyeglasses on his round face made him look like an owl. He was unsuited to military life and he knew it, but France needed men to defend her.

Though he was deployed near the front, due to his poor eyesight he was prevented from combat. He was sent to the front where he worked with the sappers, the war engineers who specialized in laying, detecting, and disarming land mines. The work required of him much manual labor and the conditions and accommodations were deplorable, especially now that the cold and wet of winter was setting in.

Messiaen was inept at mechanical things, except for the pipe organ. He even had trouble with his suitcase lock. "He can't open a can," one of his commanding officers proclaimed at roll call one morning. "*Mon Dieu!* He's blind and as coordinated as an ox! How can we trust him with a rifle and other arms, let alone allow him to carry grenades? You artists are useless on the front. They should have left you to teach music harmony to the troops and officers."

Messiaen's haversack was a collection of musical scores, everything from Bach to Berg, and his copy of the Bible and the *Imitation of Christ*. He read the musical scores constantly, fearing that if he did not he would forget his technique and even the ability to write music. He scribbled musical ideas and read musical scores to maintain his sanity and prayed the scriptures and read the *Imitation*.

He asked to be reassigned as a medical auxiliary rather than as an infantryman, but no order had come down granting his transfer. Messiaen's thoughts gamboled about nervously among his latest work for the pipe organ, an orchestral composition, the dreadful army life, and the Phoney War.

Meanwhile his heart ached for Claire and Pascal. How Claire must worry every minute of every day, wondering if the war had started or would ever start. In all of her letters the unwritten question loomed across the page: *When will you return home?* He repeatedly took out the photograph of Claire and Pascal.

Daily activities became completely different from the orderly life of which he was accustomed. While in training everything was done at prescribed times, but now as they waited out the Germans, all this had changed. The hours were mismatched; one lost track of the days, even meals did not correspond to the proper hour. There was a lot of wine and bread as they waited for the war to start. In the process of waiting, many grew bored with the whole purpose for being there. There were no passes or furloughs granted and life was lived from one shift to another.

Messiaen's world had gone from church, music lectures, and family life to days filled with the sights, sounds, smells and drudgery of military life. Laffly three-ton artillery ten-wheel tractor trucks; Somua Half-track artillery tractors; armored Somua S35 cars; Renault FT17, D1, D2, and R35 tanks; gun-carriers and infantry cargo carriers; sub-machine guns, grenades, M29 Chatellerault machine guns, the smell of diesel fuel, and all the other necessities of war weighed him down as did his kit bag. But nothing was as heavy as his loneliness and his constant concern for Claire and Pascal.

In early November he received a letter from his wife.

10 November 1939

> *Dear Oli,*
>
> *Your photo is near Jesus on the Cross so our young gentleman Pascal can, in passing, give an affectionate glance at the two people he loves. He kisses your pictures and blows you kisses. Pray war is averted and you can be home by Christmas.*
>
> *I pray there will be no more war! I said to Pascal today: 'Just you wait, my darling, when the war is over the bells in Jesus' house will ring loudly announcing peace.' And thinking about that hour of deliverance made me sob even as I spoke. I am still weeping as I write.*
>
> *Oli, you are my beloved, my reason for living. Olivier, my pet, I love you so much. May nothing make you suffer. Be happy, confident, and brave in the face of days without a letter from me. Keep your spirits up as best you can.*
>
> *I am your little Mi. xo Pascal xo*

Olivier re-read the letter from Claire and poured over the last portion in particular. He wondered what she meant by "in the face of days without a letter from me." Was it becoming too much of a strain to write a letter? The more he pondered it, the more uneasy he became. He could tell by the way her hand seemed less steady than usual and several words were crossed out and rewritten, that his absence was causing a resurgence of that melancholia to which she was so prone. Claire, whether she knew it or not, had conveyed a dismal and heavy feeling onto the page, and it soaked through the very paper itself. Olivier's hands shook as they held the letter.

He remembered the first time he saw her. She was a student from the *Schola Cantorum* and performed several violin works at a recital and he thought of her as a bird, producing such beautiful music so effortlessly, as if it was the most natural thing in the world for her to do. Her skill and interpretation of the works of Bach, Beethoven and Mozart spoke to his heart. He introduced himself to her and encouraged her to continue her studies at the Paris Conservatoire.

Over time he was smitten with her and their shared desire to compose music. He smiled to himself recalling the great surprise he and Claire brought to their friends when they announced their intention to marry. It all happened so fast that he even surprised himself when he asked her to marry. They wed in June of 1932. The two performed his *Theme and Variations for Violin and Piano* together at a public recital in November of the same year.

In 1936, as an anniversary gift, he composed *Poèmes pour Mi* — *Mi* was his pet name for Claire. They were happy and wounded with love for each other. It was a beautiful chapter of their lives.

How things had changed.

Now as he walked with the letter in his hand that evening as the sun began to set, a chill filled the air, and he thought of her as a frail bird shivering in the cold. He had only to scoop the poor creature into his hands and breathe on it to warm it, and then she would be free to fly again. And she would delight his heart and the hearts of all those around, simply by her presence, like a nightingale perched in an oak tree singing its sweet morning song.

Poor Mi! Will you ever be the same again? Will you ever be my happy little songbird? My little Mi. He wanted to cry, and as an artist he was free to do so, but as a soldier at war he fought back the tears. They made it as far as the brim of his eyes, but quickly returned to that place from which they came with a hard blink and a tight swallow.

He chose to ignore his anxious thoughts and continued to write her as normal. At Christmas his painful thoughts gave way to the joy of the season as he wrote her.

25 December 1939

Dear Mi,

I was asked to play the pipe organ on Christmas day here for the troops. The church here has an abandoned instrument, worthless really. Can you imagine the joy I experienced being able to play Bach and Widor! The soldiers enjoyed the impromptu concert I provided after Mass. Widor's Toccata can bring a smile to the most hardened heart. When I am on watch with my feet freezing to the point where they feel as if they are burning with cold in the deep snow, I often find myself singing certain of my favorite hymns and I have been going over in my head the most important parts of my latest organ work.

As you know, I finished the draft of the organ work in August while on holiday with you and Pascal at Petichet before Hitler changed our plans, but I have not been able to perfect it in my mind. It deals with the resurrection of the bodies. Will I ever be able to complete it? Will I even live to complete it, let alone perform it? I will wait and hope for all my expectations are hitched to Christian hope.

Yet how does one find work in a war — work which will allow me to continue writing and performing music? I keep my mind occupied with anything but this dreaded war-or the lack thereof. Perhaps I could be transferred to Rennes so as to work in a radio station. Oh, the ridiculous things one thinks while waiting the enemy out. Marcel Dupré may be able to secure a post for me and get me out of harm's way. I have sent him a letter asking for his assistance in the matter.

Oh, how I long to be with you and Pascal. Joyeux Noel!

All my love,

Oli

As he sealed the envelope in the privacy of the empty barracks he finally wept.

*****

The winter of 1940 was ruthlessly cold with lots of blowing and drifting snow. The strains of Tchaikovsky's First Symphony "Winter Dreams" filled Messiaen's mind, making the work of shoveling snow a bit more bearable. But this was not Tchaikovsky's wonderland of snow, but the nightmare of sinful men's own making. Even though no shots had yet been fired in the war with Germany, the present preparation for war was a horror that Messiaen loathed.

By late January 1940, Messiaen was still cutting down trees, digging holes, and pushing wheelbarrows full of dirt, slush, and snow. He lamented his bruised hands and blackened fingers, believing that they had been created for the keys of an organ and piano and never intended for such harsh labor or to become mere instruments of war.

Miserable and exhausted, he asked again to work with the medics as a nurse or an orderly. His commanding officer finally recognized that Messiaen's gifts lay elsewhere, so he was transferred to an ambulance unit and made an orderly. He was then sent north to Verdun.

*****

Chapter 3

Verdun

In February 1940, after establishing himself at Verdun with 10,000 troops, Olivier Messiaen met Corporal Etienne Pasquier, the conductor of the French military orchestra, *theâtre aux armées*, at the citadel of Vauban. Etienne Pasquier was a handsome dark-haired Frenchman, 35 years of age with a contagious smile and a positive personality. Under his black military beret, his khaki uniform was perfectly pressed and starched.

Messiaen met Pasquier outside the snowy citadel the day he was reassigned to Verdun.

"I was told of your arrival, professor," the finely dressed corporal said as he stopped Messiaen.

Messiaen saluted his superior officer. "Corporal."

"Corporal Etienne Pasquier," Pasquier identified himself with a smile.

"*Etienne* Pasquier of the Pasquier Trio?" Messiaen's eyes brightened.

"*Oui*," he said, "but do let us get out of this miserable weather."

The two men then entered into the cavernous underground fortress.

"I have heard broadcasts of your Trio," Messiaen said, as they continued on their way.

"Yes, my brothers and I were quite successful before war was declared, but you are the composer, professor, organist, and pianist, Olivier Messiaen. Your work is well known and much discussed."

"Which, to the military, means little," Messiaen said with a sigh.

"Well, at least you are no longer at Metz," Pasquier answered. "I am honored to serve France along with you. Here we can utilize your musical talents."

"Thank God." Messiaen made the sign of the cross.

"If there is a God," Pasquier questioned, adjusting his beret.

"You are not a believer?"

"I was raised a Catholic, but I prefer the more fashionable moniker of agnostic. The inhumanity of war eliminated much of the faith I was taught as a child. If there is a God, would he allow such evil?"

Messiaen said nothing as Pasquier showed him to his quarters and led him to the large underground mess hall.

"There is another musician I would like for you to meet," Pasquier said. "Henri Akoka."

Henri Akoka was arguing with a group of soldiers at table when Pasquier introduced him to Messiaen.

"Henri, this is Olivier Messiaen," Pasquier nodded to Messiaen, "the composer from Paris. He has been assigned here as an orderly."

Pasquier then motioned to Henri Akoka. "Olivier, Henri is a clarinetist from the *Orchestre National de la Radio* in Paris."

Akoka placed his lit cigarette in his mouth and shook Messiaen's hand. His olive military beret sat atop his head askew.

"Yes," Akoka said, "I have seen you in Paris and even attended one of your concerts, but we have never met. Your music is...how shall I say...? Different."

"*Merci*,...I think," Messiaen smiled as they broke off their handshake.

Messiaen studied Henri Akoka's swarthy facial features. He had the look of a Mediterranean. His eyes were small, dark, and deep-set; his nose was large and spread across his face, falling away into sunken cheeks. What hair stuck out from under his beret was frizzy. But what was most notable about Henri Akoka was the clarinet that he proudly carried under his left arm.

"I was drafted into the service and sent to the citadel of Vauban where I was to play clarinet for the orchestra, *theâtre aux armées*," Akoka said as he removed his cigarette.

Messiaen shook his head in understanding.

In the course of their conversation, Akoka revealed that he was a 28 year old Jew of Algerian descent and a Trotskyite.

"Leon Trostsky, the Russian Bolshevik revolutionary and Marxist, was exiled from Russia in 1929 by Joseph Stalin," Akoka continued. "Trotsky maintains that the practice of communism must extend to a worldwide revolution instead of applying socialism in only one country."

Messiaen was not sympathetic to Communism.

The next time Messiaen met Akoka was again in the mess hall where Akoka was arguing with Pasquier and some other officers at dinner.

"In order for Communism to work, it must extend to the entire world," Akoka vociferously articulated his point as he smoked his cigarette intensely, the ash visibly growing longer as he inhaled.

Akoka then unexpectedly drew Messiaen into the conversation as the latter was seating himself at table.

"Now here is a real revolutionary. The radical leftist musician, Olivier Messiaen!"

"I do not advocate revolution," Messiaen argued, taken aback by the comment.

"Ridiculous," Akoka laughed. "Your entire oeuvre is based on musical revolution. Haven't you listened to your music? It certainly isn't classical."

Messiaen was silent.

Pasquier patted him on the back. "Henri's got you there, Olivier."

They all laughed.

Messiaen finally felt that he was among kindred souls, save their religious and political views. He was familiar enough with artists and the kind of men who could respect one another despite their differences.

*****

As the winter dragged on, the morale of the French soldiers was at its lowest ebb. There was apathy, disobedience, and a lack of discipline in the ranks. Many openly dismissed the French military leadership and drunkenness continued to be a problem among many of the men. Some of the men began to fight amongst themselves as they gambled while others wenched their way through some of the neighboring villages.

However, Messiaen's own personal struggles seemed to far outweigh a few angry soldiers, and even though his friendship with Pasquier and Akoka made the mundane military life more bearable, his heart was heavy.

After supper one evening in the mess hall as Messiaen scribbled some musical ideas, he lost himself in thought as he watched one of the soldiers cleaning the tables and doing the dishes. The sights and sounds of his own kitchen flooded his heart. Claire was foremost in his thoughts. The absence of letters from Claire conjured the ghosts of her past once again. In the time he had been away, he had had ample time to ruminate upon her condition.

Yes, he had seen it but he couldn't admit it. Others had asked him if she was all right and he assured them she was fine though he knew otherwise. The memories of her miscarriages haunted her. After one of her miscarriages prior to the birth of Pascal, she exclaimed that she would die if she couldn't give him a child, so distraught over not being able to carry a child, not being able to be the wife Olivier deserved, or fulfilling her role as a mother.

The struggle led to a growing spiritual desert for her since many of her friends were having babies. Her heart was breaking. At times she didn't even want to go to Mass; her only prayer was her presence, for she would leave the church as barren as she came. After the third miscarriage she sat in the rocking chair, weeping over the empty baby crib that she had arranged in the corner of their bedroom and cradled the baby's quilt her mother had made for her. She blamed herself for the miscarriages and believed she would never give birth. Olivier was helpless to assuage her grief and pain for he was grieving the miscarriages as well.

Finally when she conceived again, they waited to tell anyone for fear of yet another miscarriage. But when she entered the sixth month, she could no longer conceal the fact that she was pregnant. When young Pascal was born it was a radiant period of great joy for both Claire and Olivier.

Yet Claire soon entered another phase of melancholia and closed herself off from others, even friends, and began to decline offers for friends to visit. Ever since giving birth to Pascal, Messiaen had noted her depression; her emotional frailty; her grief and post-partum blues; her fatigue; her insomnia and nighttime bouts of crying; a decreased interest in her music; her doubts concerning her ability to be a good mother; her headaches; her increasing irritability, forgetfulness and trouble concentrating; and her loss of a desire for sexual intimacy, which was so unlike her since she and Olivier had been passionate lovers.

Weaning Pascal was very difficult for her and she felt guilty that Pascal would likely be an only child and regretted that she couldn't give Olivier more children.

Despite all his worry, Messiaen was silent about his growing concern for Claire. He tried to dismiss it as the sorrow of her miscarriages, yet in her face and in her eyes he sensed the same melancholy of his mother, the same doubt and lack of hope, a deeper pain. He couldn't admit it to himself. But now in the toilsome hours of war preparations his heart sank as he thought of his lovely Claire who was wispily slipping away from him. The doctor said it was due to a hormonal imbalance that would likely correct itself, but nearly two years later there was no sign of improvement.

Now the mere thought of Claire being all alone caused Messiaen to want to forget it all. It was all too painful knowing that he couldn't be there to help her with Pascal. He lifted her and his son in prayer.

His thoughts turned to his faith and the words of Christ to the disciples on the road to Emmaus were being asked of him as well: "Did you not know that the Messiah must suffer and die?"

He looked down at his music sheet and the notes he had written. In his music his anger and anxiety came through: chaos and rage, dissonance and upheaval. Yes, he was devout, but he wrestled with his certainty. His faith gave him reasons to believe, and though his faith did not answer all of his questions, his faith did give him the hope to live the questions, to embrace his uncertainty, doubts and pain.

The words of the Savior were on his lips: *Take up your cross and follow me.*

*****

With the advent of spring, the gray of winter and melting snow gave way to the green grass, sprouting leaves, and red, pink, purple, and yellow of flowers. By March of 1940 many French — both soldiers and civilians — thought that there would be no armed conflict, but rather that the differences among France, Britain and Germany would be settled diplomatically.

Corporal Etienne Pasquier, the optimistic agnostic cellist, was Messiaen's commanding officer. Pasquier managed for the two to be assigned night patrol duties together so they could discuss their common interests and help make the war, or the lack thereof, more tolerable.

One such April morning, right before sunrise, the two were talking.

"Olivier, you are such a solitary man" Pasquier said as he lit a cigarette and took a long drag.

"*Oui*. I have always been self-directed, independent. I suffer from an unknown, distant music."

"Excuse me?" he removed his cigarette from his mouth and exhaled a column of smoke.

"It was a line from a poem that my mother wrote for me, while I was yet unborn." Messiaen adjusted the rifle on his shoulder.

"Is she still alive?"

"No, she died in 1927," Messiaen said, holding back his emotion. "She was a devoted mother. I inherited her work ethic and creativity. You know, even though she is dead, I still believe she is present to me, guiding me in a way."

"Was she musically gifted?" Pasquier asked.

With the mention of his mother he was haunted by her melancholia, atheism, depression, and lack of hope, and was distracted from the question about her musical ability.

"No. No," Messiaen answered, adjusting his round framed eyeglasses upon his face. "Neither she nor my father. I taught myself to play my aunt's old piano when I was seven years old. I loved melody. When I was ten years old my music teacher gave me a vocal score of Claude Debussy's *Pelléas et Mélisande*, and it made such an impression upon me that I decided to become a composer."

"Seriously?" Pasquier looked down his nose at Messiaen.

"*Oui*. I entered the Paris Conservatory that same year. Debussy's work was a veritable bomb in the hands of a mere child."

"The only bomb with which I would trust you," laughed Pasquier as he returned the cigarette to his mouth.

30

Messiaen laughed and continued discussing the influences upon his music. He loved the stained glass windows of *Sainte Chappelle* in Paris. "I was overwhelmed by the colors and light. Just as you must experience these windows in the light, so must you feel music and truly listen to it, truly hear it – and be shocked by the sound. I see notes as color."

He had never played the organ until 1927, but by 1929 he had mastered the instrument under the guidance of Marcel Dupré. In 1934 he began composing for the organ and had studied the organ works of Charles Tournemire, the French composer and organist, most famous for his improvisations rooted in Gregorian chant. Charles Marie Widor and Louis Vierne were notable influences as well. He had even studied the Hindu rhythmician Carngadeva.

"As the conditions of life become more and more hard, mechanical and impersonal, music must ceaselessly bring to those who love it its spiritual violence and its courageous reactions. If we're musicians, then we've got to play and practice. The sheer beauty of our musical ideas will get us notice. If not, then we will still know that we did something important, all for the glory of God. *Ad majorem Dei gloriam!*

"My faith teaches me that all we do either gives glory and honor to God or not. Some of my critics have said, 'It certainly isn't Bach or Mozart.' To which I reply, 'It isn't supposed to be Bach or Mozart.' Then they say, 'Well, it's not even Debussy or Ravel.' To which I say, 'No. It is Messiaen.'" He laughed.

Pasquier laughed along with him.

Messiaen talked about his wife and son, but did not reveal any of his concerns for her health; he mainly spoke of his most recent musical works, before being called up for service.

"I wrote *Poèmes pour Mi* for my wife, originally for voice and piano, but then I scored it for orchestra the next year. The piano version of *Poèmes pour Mi* is free of a time signature and bar lines, reflecting my love for plainchant; expressive melismas, several notes given for every syllable of the text at the end of each sentence.

"In 1938 I wrote *Chants de terre et de ciel*, after our son was born. It is a paean to the sacramental love of marriage and parenthood. I truly believe, with all my heart, that the life of the Holy Trinity is reflected in the love between husband and wife and in their gift of children."

*****

Messiaen attended Easter Mass and abhorred the fact that French Catholics were poised to kill German Catholics, and vice versa. *Christians ready to kill fellow Christians on Easter?* The insanity of it all seemed too absurd to be true.

Spring 1940 unfolded in every bloom, blossom, and leaf which gave Messiaen and the other soldiers some glimmer of hope amid the grey bleakness of a long winter of a war that never came.

The fresh scent of spring with rainfall, warm sun, wildflowers, and white and yellow sweet honeysuckle fragranced the April air. Sights and sounds of bees and the season's first butterflies and the beauty of budding flowers and greening trees and ever-increasing signs of new life served as a great contradiction as human beings continued their build-up for war, preparing to maim, kill, and destroy.

The bouquet of wildflowers and honeysuckle reminded Olivier of one of the many weeks he and Claire spent on holiday picnicking, enjoying the beauties of nature, basking in the sun, breathing the mountain air, listening to and watching the various birds, her in his arms and he in hers, the two intertwined in the rapturous, selfless love of marriage.

Meanwhile, Etienne Pasquier and Olivier Messiaen had become close friends in the past few months. As the two men served night guard duty together, often a nightingale would break the silence of the night and sing his repertoire of songs and calls.

Then by morning Messiaen was like a child on Christmas morning as the first streaks of dawn graced the skies and the nightingale calls gave way to a veritable chorus of birds assembled as an orchestra.

"Look! There! Dawn is breaking! Listen! The peeps and tweets will begin. In the stillness a small bird will announce the opening pitch like a conductor!" Messiaen explained, as if he could communicate with the birds. "Listen to them banter back and forth. It is the orchestra of God.

They're giving each other the day's assignments in song. While we're here prepared to blow each other to bits, the birds are singing a wonderful harmony without meter, without measure, without time! And then tonight they'll reunite at the vesper hour at which time they will give thanks to God and recount to one another all the wonders they saw during the day.

"If only men could learn to live as the birds and trust in their heavenly Father. '*Behold the birds of the air...they neither toil nor spin, they do not gather wheat into barns, yet their heavenly Father feeds them.*' Is there any wonder Saint Francis of Assisi loved the birds so? He preached to them, you know. Well, the birds preach to me. Birds know no borders, they are free and they sing – they rise early to sing like the monks and nuns, to sing God's praise and they are provided for. Birds are little prophets of immaterial joy. Why can't men and women, created in the image of God, learn to imitate the birds?"

"Olivier, you are a beautiful man," Pasquier replied, lighting a cigarette. "How in heaven's name did your superiors ever approve of you being sent to the front?"

"God's providence is far greater than our human schemes. I am here for some higher purpose, though I have no idea what that purpose is. I truly believe this." He adjusted his glasses and held them halfway down his nose.

"*Oui*," Pasquier answered, as he held his cigarette and blew the smoke into the air. "I know you do."

On 7 May 1940, just as France relaxed it restriction against allowing her troops to go on furloughs, Hitler ordered that the siege on Western Europe begin. The *sitzkrieg*, "sitting war" had come to an end.

*****

Chapter 4

The Clarinet

Belgium and Holland were attacked. In France, in the middle of the day on 13 May, hundreds of fighter planes and Stuka dive bombers bombed and strafed French positions near the Ardennes. France's military leaders relied on infantry hunkered down in trenches and the generals discounted the concern that Panzer tanks would roll over the French forces. With Germany on the offensive, Pasquier ordered his unit to keep their rifles, machine guns, and gas masks with them at all times.

Some of the younger men in their company wanted to take the fight to the Germans. However, the Germans were bringing the fight to them.

"I told you Hitler would never negotiate," Henri Akoka proclaimed one evening in the barracks as he practiced a melody on his clarinet. "The reason he waited to attack now is because everyone thought the war was phoney, and those eight months gave him time to build up his forces and get everything in place. Are we French ever the idiots? You should have listened to us."

"*Us?*" asked Messiaen, as he busily worked on a musical idea.

"The Trotskyites. When Chamberlain signed his deal with Hitler, Trotsky warned that this would lead directly to the pact between Hitler and Stalin. We were the only ones condemning Hitler. We warned France!"

"*Communism?*" Pasquier entered the conversation, leaning against Messiaen's bunk.

"The Communists in Russia are not true Marxists. Stalin betrayed the Revolution," Akoka waved his arms, his clarinet under his right arm.

"But what of religious freedom?" Messiaen asked, still writing, looking over the rims of his glasses halfway down his nose.

"The worker state has rejected the church and all its ceremony," Akoka answered, searching his pockets for a cigarette. "The citizens have the right to live without the tyranny of mysterious gestures and refrains of men in cassocks and vestments."

"Yes, the state may have declared that," Messiaen said, putting his pencil down, "but the people are still religious."

"Custom finds it harder to discard ceremony than the state," Akoka retorted, discovering his cigarette pack. "Religion is the opiate of the people."

"Or is materialism the opiate of the people?" Messiaen asked, his right hand to his chin in a philosophical pose.

"These people have no material comfort," Akoka said, tapping a cigarette out and putting it in between his lips. "They are poor. Religion feeds on the poor's frustration with capitalism and gives them hope that if they simply pray long and hard enough they will be delivered from their conditions. If not here, then in another world."

"Is that it?" Messiaen laughed. "Prayer is the best use of our time."

"But most people are too busy working that they've no time to pray," Akoka flicked his lighter.

"If we're too busy to pray, then we're too busy," Messiaen shook his head and looked away.

"A pious thought, but religious doctrine perpetuates a fictitious knowledge of the universe," Akoka argued, successfully lighting his smoke.

"But what of your faith?" Messiaen asked, furrowing his brow.

"*Oui*. I am Jewish," he said before inhaling on the cigarette, "but I discarded the miraculous long ago."

"But what of your family? Are your parents religious?"

"Yes. Very much so as I am sure your parents are." Akoka exhaled the smoke in the air.

"Actually, they were not." Messiaen's eyes returned to Akoka. "I was born a believer, it seems."

"Then you have a mental illness," Akoka harrumphed.

"Yes, perhaps," Messiaen laughed. "I believe I was born out of time, like Saint Paul."

"He was a Jew, you know."

"As was Christ," Messiaen passionately replied as he placed his music sheet and pencil in his haversack.

"Tell that to the Germans," Akoka said with a smirk, his cigarette dangling from his mouth.

"You two make this war bearable," Pasquier smiled. "Let's go outside for some fresh air." Akoka and Messiaen followed him through one of the underground halls to the door opening to the outside. The men beheld the late evening sun and breathed in the fresh May air.

"Here you are, the quintessential twentieth century composer, avant-garde, and yet you are religious, and a Catholic at that," Akoka continued the banter. "Wasn't Hitler raised Catholic?"

"His faith is in the Reich and his Nazi beliefs," Messiaen adamantly replied.

"*Oui*," Akoka nodded.

"And if Hitler was a faithful Catholic," Messiaen asked, "would I be here in Verdun with you?"

"See? Trotsky has united us." Akoka laughed as he smoked his cigarette and leaned against one of the army ambulances.

"In Christ our faiths are united." Messiaen smiled.

"Yes, your faith in God and my faith in Man," Akoka replied.

"*Non*, Jesus the Jew."

"You are clever, my friend," Akoka said as he tapped the ashes of his cigarette on the fender of the truck he was leaning on. "And if Christianity were true, would one Christian nation raise its sword against another?" He paused awaiting a reply from Messiaen or Pasquier but neither replied. "Thus I prove my point. And who do these leaders blame for their woes?" Akoka asked with a flourish, his cigarette still between his fingers and his clarinet under his right arm. "Why, the Jews, of course." He returned the cigarette to his mouth and took a long final toke and exhaled dramatically.

"Of course. The Jews." Pasquier replied, looking at both men.

"*Oui*," Akoka acknowledged Pasquier. "We are not called *The Chosen People* for nothing. Chosen to be the world's whipping boy."

Silence fell among them as Akoka flicked his spent cigarette away only to pull out another.

"I fear that the anti-Semitism of Nazism is a harbinger of far worse things to befall the civilized world." Akoka worked to light his cigarette with his clarinet still under his arm.

"Even worse than total war?" Pasquier asked.

"Yes. There is a fear of another pogrom against all Jews, far more terrible than *Kristallnacht*. Many of our people have been placed in concentration camps and work camps, reduced to slave laborers by Capitalist pigs." Akoka closed his eyes as he puffed on his cigarette.

Messiaen was momentarily distracted by several song birds and a cuckoo heralding the arrival of spring. He turned to Akoka and changed the subject. "Do you ever play that clarinet, or do you simply carry it around as a prop while you expound upon your Trotskyite revolutionary theories?"

"Ah, you too are also a revolutionary," Akoka said, pulling his clarinet out from under his arm as if to play. "I have heard your music. The bourgeoisie French have no respect for you just as they have no respect for the proletariat. So you see, you and the artists have much in common with our people. You would make a fine Trotskyite."

"*Oui*," Messiaen explained. "There are those in the Church and the music world who would agree that I am a revolutionary and have come to destroy the very foundations of faith and music."

"Where does that put you in relation to Nazism?" Akoka asked.

"Hitler claims that the Roman Catholics who oppose him are the tools of Bolshevism," Messiaen explained. "So I suppose that does put us in the same camp."

"Man will not be free until he is freed from his degrading dependence upon nature and free from all mystery, especially the mystery of religion," Akoka said.

"I couldn't disagree more," Messiaen asserted, "But I still like you."

"Democracy and all its talk of liberty, equality and fraternity, is but a slave of capitalism. My faith is——" Akoka said before being cut off mid-sentence by Etienne Pasquier.

"*My* faith is in wine, women and song," Pasquier declared, interrupting the philosophical-socio-political-religious dispute between Akoka and Messiaen. "You men are depressing the hell out of me. Let's hear some music and I'll fetch some wine. *Vive la France!* Certainly we can drink to the women in our lives. It's spring! The flowers are in bloom!"

"*Oui*, my friend," Akoka replied, holding his clarinet out at arms' length. "What would you like to hear?"

"You know, seeing you with your clarinet set me to thinking of a piece for solo clarinet," Messiaen's eyes were alight with excitement as he fumbled with his haversack.

"What is in that kit of yours?" Pasquier asked as he lit a cigarette. "You carry that thing with you wherever you go."

"Do you ever rest?" Akoka asked Messiaen. "You are forever writing something."

"My work is my joy," Messiaen winked at Akoka. "Seriously, you inspired me to work on piece for clarinet."

"What is it?" Akoka asked.

"I have been listening to the birds, jotting down a few notes," he revealed his notebook from his haversack. "It's not much."

"Let me see," Akoka said, taking a few moments to look over the score. "Much of it is missing a time signature."

"The music of the future will have no time. I am toying with new modes, new rhythms, some based on the neumes of Gregorian chant."

"*Plainchant?*"

"And birdsong. They are the world's first musicians, *non?* Music is music. Just as religious matters include everything, so music should as well."

"Let me try this," Akoka said as Messiaen held the music sheet in front of him.

The piece started out slow, but then Akoka's fingers rippled across the keys as the notes trilled and jumped high and low.

"'*Bathed in sunshine, like a bird, very free in movement,*'" Akoka read Messiaen's notes above the four bars of the *presque vif* section. "I like it, but this is a challenge. I like a challenge. I should like to play this another day, when it is more polished, let us say, and when you have *more time.*"

"Time?" Messiaen's eyebrows raised above the horn-rims of his glasses at the unintended double entendre.

"It's too difficult to play as it is."

"You will have to blame that on the nightingale and the blackbird that inspired it – and this interminable waiting for war."

"What is it called?"

"I'm not sure. *Flight over Time? French Nightingale's victory over the Nazi Eagle?* We shall see."

"You are a work of art, Olivier," Pasquier laughed.

The men were abruptly startled by the wail of air raid sirens. At first none of the men moved, so accustomed were they to the threat of war and routine air raid sirens. The commanders alerted the men that the warning was real, yet it didn't seem real until they began to hear explosions.

At first the sounds seemed innocent enough, as if from a far off thunderstorm, but this was no natural phenomenon: this was the long anticipated war. Soon the wail of air raid sirens was accompanied by the screeching of Stuka bombers.

The commanding officers began shouting orders to the men and chaos ensued.

"Luftwaffe! Incoming aircraft!" one man yelled.

"Lights out!" another shouted. "Man the anti-aircraft guns!"

The strafing machine gun fire came first followed by the whistling and thud of bombs.

This was no dream, but a nightmare about to be exacted upon the French.

*****

"I am convinced that joy exists,
convinced that the invisible exists
more than the visible,
joy is beyond sorrow,
beauty is beyond horror."

- Olivier Messiaen

Chapter 5

Blitzkrieg

May 1940

The German Luftwaffe darkened the skies with Messerschmitt single seat bombers and the two man Stuka dive bombers. The Stuka bombers were equipped with screaming sirens that only sounded when the planes dove down, instilling a sinister terror in all who heard.

The Stuka bombers dove to less than a thousand feet to bomb and strafe with machine gun fire, all the while shrieking their harpy-like, howling, maddening, demonic sirens to the rhythm of exploding bullets: the shrill whine of banshees.

The pilots released their bombs and they whistled down. The detonation was deafening and mud and dirt splattered everywhere. The explosion of flame and smoke, and shower of debris was followed by more screeching and whistling, and more violent bursts of thunderous detonations and discharges and more flame, smoke, dirt, mud, and debris.

"Off the road, off the road!" came the order from one of the French commanders. "Fire, fire, get those guns in the air! Shoot! Shoot! Bring those Stukas down!!"

"Where the hell is our air force?" many of the men called out.

The wailing screams of the Stukas was incessant and deafening. With each whistling bomb every man wondered if it was on top of him. The descent of bombs and the rain of shells and bullets throttled the men into confusion.

The klaxon horns continued to rise and fall, warning both the living and the dead as shells sparkled through the night.

Messiaen shook with stiffness, his legs as if frozen, his thoughts unclear. *What would become of his wife, his son, and his music if he were killed?*

Ever since September of the year before he had merely speculated about death; now he was on the edge of Golgotha, the place of the skull.

It was all a trap. The German army had attacked Holland and Belgium and was now moving into Luxembourg. The Allies were moving into Belgium, but the Germans were moving west to take the coast along the channel, and southwest, planning an attack through the Ardennes Forest. The French military brass said this couldn't happen. Yet the Allied air fields had been attacked and many Allied planes were lost. Of the ones that made it to the skies, many were shot down by the Luftwaffe.

Reports came in that the Germans were crossing the Meuse River. French gunners were in retreat as Panzer divisions were on the move back west while the Luftwaffe covered their advance by air. This was blitzkrieg: lightning war.

Messiaen's services as an orderly with the medical unit were now put to use. He had plenty of work in his makeshift hospital, an ambulance, and kit full of bandages, iodine, and other assorted medical supplies. The wounded and maimed needed comfort and care, but his ambulance stretcher was a funeral bier for half his casualties. The dead were merely carried away, either hurriedly buried or left to rot, receiving none of the Rites of the Church or synagogue.

The strafing and explosions finally subsided as the soldiers and civilians waited for the screaming bombers to end their reign of terror. The poor French civilians that Messiaen witnessed were dumbfounded. Especially sad were the elderly, experiencing the third major war of their lifetime: the Franco-Prussian War, the Great War, and, now, the Nazi Aggression.

The sight and sound and smell of death and destruction was everywhere. The despondent faces, hollow glances, vacant stares; broken noses, bruised and scorched faces; the maimed, blind, lame; legless, armless, deafened, dumb; bewildered, confused, dizzy; hungry, thirsty, dirty, and exhausted: exiles in their own land. Though the first wave of the German offensive was over, they feared the worst was yet to come.

How many civilians had Messiaen watched as they stumbled through the rubble of what had once been their homes? The soldiers were not the only ones with forsaken hopes, broken bones, and charred flesh.

Through the fire and smoke Messiaen found Corporal Etienne Pasquier and Henri Akoka. All three had been spared in the attack; Akoka was still clutching his clarinet and Messiaen his medical kit and haversack. Pasquier and his men regrouped with one of the unit commanders. Messiaen stumbled through the darkness shaking with fear.

At night the smokers cupped their hands around the lit end of their cigarette. Even the glowing end of a cigarette could be seen from a distance and German snipers were liable to be anywhere.

"The Germans have taken Holland and are moving through Belgium," one of the commanding officers told the men. "The Allied forces are in retreat."

Meanwhile, the din of exploding shells to the north distracted Messiaen from composing and kept him on the edge of anxiety. In a strange way he feared more for the loss of his music than the loss of his own life.

German raids were sporadic for a while as reports came out of Belgium and Dunkirk. Belgium had been conquered and Dunkirk was a disaster. The Germans had easily broken through the Maginot line breaching the Ardennes forest at Sedan and crossing the Meuse River. The Panzer divisions were everywhere and the skies belonged to the Germans as well.

"*Mon Dieu*, we're taking a beating," Akoka said, leaning against a trench wall smoking a cigarette.

"There's nothing left to bomb or anyone to kill, according to the reports," Pasquier said. "The Germans really did it to us this time. The Brits have all gone home. We are all alone," Pasquier said, working to light his cigarette from behind his cupped hands. "Hitler's revenge."

Messiaen said nothing, somberly, soberly recalling all the devastation. Thoughts of his wife and son brought tears to his eyes.

When Sunday came, the church bells of Verdun rang. Messiaen decided to go to Mass at the closest church. Several of the soldiers went with him. The church's ceiling over the nave, having been pierced asunder by a bomb in a previous air raid, hung down and revealed the blue sky above. Many of the pews were destroyed, requiring some of the people to stand; a few people were sitting on the splintered timbers.

Messiaen was weighed down with his rifle, gas mask, helmet, and bandoleer of ammunition.

After Mass, Messiaen asked to play the church organ which, happily, was undamaged by the bomb. To his relief his musical idea came to mind: *Combat de la mort et de la vie* (the combat of death and life). He worked it out on the aging instrument, much to the chagrin of the parishioners. The music was as dissonant and chaotic as were their lives in the wake of German attacks, yet as long as he was alive he would compose and play.

Messiaen cut short his miniature concert when, over the echo of the pipe organ, the wail of air raid sirens were heard. As everyone abandoned the church and sought shelter, he heard the screeching, harpy shrieks of more incoming Stuka bombers.

Messiaen darted down the stairs of the choir loft, ran back to the citadel, dodging bullets and bombs, and crawled his way back to the bomb shelter. When he rejoined his compatriots, Etienne Pasquier and Henri Akoka chastised him for his indiscretion.

"What were you thinking, Oli?" Pasquier asked, pulling him to safety.

Henri Akoka simply shook his head as he smoked a cigarette. "You are one f—ing lucky man."

Messiaen could not put his thoughts and feelings into words.

His commanding officer sought him out as well. "Soldier, if we were not under attack, I'd place you in solitary confinement!" His words were as visible with saliva as they were audible and angry.

Messiaen felt alone in his desire for God and longing to express himself and his faith though music.

In the meantime, the German forces that had breached the Ardennes and crossed the Meuse River were moving northward toward Verdun. Another division was heading south to Verdun. If the reports were correct, the Germans would be hitting them with a huge force of tanks, men, and planes. The fortress at Verdun would fail. Pasquier's unit was ordered to retreat to Metz.

The French soldiers were trapped between Panzer divisions, cut off from the western supply line and they were now moving south and southeast toward Metz. Messiaen and his unit were at Metz when the bombing began. Metz was burning and being shelled mercilessly. Many of the French troops fled to Toul, but it was futile: the Germans had breached the Maginot Line and were everywhere.

In the midst of the chaos that ensued there were orders for their unit to move south along the Maginot Line to Epinal, but the Germans had broken through the defenses there and the line was not to be defended. Between Metz and Toul the battle waged and the French soon realized they were defeated. Many soldiers began to desert and head west. The bombing raids and tanks closed in on Messiaen, Pasquier and Akoka, who now found themselves alone in the midst of Germans.

Emotions ran high, and though no one said it, every man feared that it was either kill or be killed. Upon seeing a fellow soldier struck down dead, Henri Akoka exclaimed, "That poor son-of-a-bitch didn't make it. Well, that's not going to happen to me."

"Luftwaffe! Panzers!" Pasquier yelled.

"Nazi bastards!" was Akoka's refrain.

A cacophony of noise beat steadfastly: grinding of tanks, whistling and exploding bombshells, the rat-a-tat-tat of machine gun fire, anti-aircraft guns, discharging turrets, grenades, and explosions everywhere.

Messiaen's ears rang; he and the other men were being compassed about. Now Messiaen knew firsthand why his father never talked about his experience in the Great War. He gagged from the pungent stench of burnt and rotting flesh and sight of mangled limbs, ripped abdomens, and bloodied corpses. There were boots with legs still in them, a helmet with the man's head inside, a severed body, solitary detached limbs, a decapitated tank gunner, scattered canteens, knapsacks, cigarettes, photographs, and letters from home scattered to the wind.

All along the route, row after row of overturned tanks, destroyed trucks, burnt half-track artillery tractors, bombed armored cars, abandoned gun-carriers and forsaken gear and equipment. Littering the roads and ditches were the bodies of French men: husbands, fathers, uncles, fiancés, and lovers. Yet there was no time to stop and bury the dead; sadly, no time for a Requiem, either.

The Nazis were dividing and conquering, splitting the French troops, separating the leaders from their men and cutting off all communication among the French soldiers. The leveling of all buildings in sight, the path of destruction left by tanks, half-standing skeletons of buildings, hollowed-out shells, burnt, smoldering, or still burning. The homes looked like doll houses sliced in two, the residents trapped on second floors, amidst the rubble, or others crawling out of collapsed structures. Of course, they were the lucky ones; many other unfortunate souls, men, women, and children, were stiff, charred corpses.

The Germans invaded with great speed and great force. The Panzers were numerous and swift while the French ground troops were either being destroyed or forced to surrender. The few French planes in the air were being shot down by the Luftwaffe. The walking wounded were moving targets while the casualties were likely left for dead. The absolute chaos and confusion left many of the French soldiers scrambling for cover as they studied their maps and sought desperately to regroup.

An ethereal fog of clouds and smoke enveloped them as the sun broke over the horizon of splintered trees. The birds sang as if everything was as it had been at the first moment of creation, yet sin had destroyed the beauty of this French garden.

One madman's desire for war had led a nation to madness and plunged a continent into tumult. Though the men were in retreat, there was nowhere to go; the Germans were everywhere.

Food was scarce, possessions were scattered, civilians were trickling into their encampment begging for food and shelter; many women and children were despondent. The French had been reduced to refugees in their own country. Many were so disoriented they didn't know where they were, especially after so many of the towns had been bombed beyond recognition. It seemed all of northeastern France was burning.

As the French soldiers made their way south along the Maginot Line, they kept their eyes on No Man's Land and the Siegfried Line. The sound of nature, insects, the nightingale, and the song thrush was displaced by the menacing harpies from on high and the advancing German monster of war on the ground. The overwhelming power of armored cars and tanks, fast, large, and firing tanks, with aircraft diving down to the treetops, was horrifying. The sheer terror of the screaming Stukas caused many of the soldiers to surrender, old and young alike.

Near Messiaen, one of the French officer's leg was blown off by a Stuka bomb; several soldiers were strafed with machine-gun fire as others were bombed into oblivion. The groping German tanks gnashed the earth and smashed trees beneath them, their turrets belching fire and blasting explosives, with shrapnel, stone, and metal flying everywhere. Dirt rained down and dust became the men's bread by day and tears their drink by night.

More bodies were scattered for the carrion crows, hawks, and vultures. From under a blanket a man stirred; his back was stabbed full of shrapnel. Another man had no arm and half of his face was blown off.

The miserable nights were filled with machine gun fire, the grinding sound of tanks and the piercing scream of Stukas overhead, bombshells bursting all about them, dropping for hours all through the day and night, and each whistle, each cannon blast, each turret a lethal charge that could mean instant death. The fog of sulfur, caustic smoke of gunpowder, and acrid malodor of decomposing and burnt flesh made Messiaen vomit. *Bombing raids on civilians! Mon Dieu! What barbarism!* Messiaen shouted aloud.

Messiaen was too angry to cry. His goal was to simply survive.

The Luftwaffe bombers strafed and bombed a path for the German troops, and then the sound of tanks was heard again, this time louder and louder. The trucks and tanks both began closing in on the fleeing French soldiers and civilians; a clatter and roar of trucks and engines, ever pursuing them. The roads and ditches were filled with columns of refugees. Some of the battle weary didn't even seek refuge but appeared to be inviting death, as if their end would be a welcome relief from the hell they were living.

"We're out of ammunition! No grenades!" one of the soldiers to Messiaen's left called out.

"Get rid of any souvenirs you may have gotten off of dead Germans!" Pasquier ordered. "If they catch you with any of their medals, you'll be shot on sight!"

Messiaen, Pasquier, and Akoka had refused to engage in that morbid act of the senselessness of war.

"They're coming! I see them!" Akoka said, ducking down with his clarinet under his arm.

"You have no rifle or grenades, but you still have your clarinet," Pasquier quietly said to Akoka, observing the musical instrument in the midst of the confusion.

"*Oui*, music is the most powerful weapon for peace," Akoka whispered.

Messiaen smiled and nodded. It was a wonderful thought that momentarily displaced the horror.

The Stukas returned and the bombs started falling again. This time there were both Messerschmitts and Stukas. Men killing men was horrible enough, but with modern warfare it was done with the push of a lever or the opening of a hatch in the belly of a plane. Such a sickening sight of human carnage. Who would answer for all the senseless violence, killing a fellow member of the human race, all in the name of war, but murder by any other name? Bodies strewn as far as the eye could see; the trenches full of bloody corpses. Entire towns and villages reduced to broken stones, twisted metal, and splintered, smoldering wood, draped in the fetid funk of death.

The ambulances were full of causalities. French armored cars, half-tracks, troop carriers, and tanks were abandoned, destroyed, and burning; the smell of diesel fumes, the stinging fumes of sulfur, explosives, gun smoke, and unyielding magnesium were in the air as a phosphorous haze fogged the air and burned Messiaen and his companions' nostrils.

Messiaen recalled the last time Frenchmen had warred with Germany. Why would this time be any different, no matter who won? Were there really winners in a war? Who lost? The poor, the refugee, the women and children whose husbands and fathers would never return? Many were reported as missing in action, their bodies mere carrion for the beasts of the forest and birds of the air, crushed under the treads of armored tanks and trampling boots of the Nazis.

Messiaen had bloody blisters on his bruised feet and both his feet and legs were in great pain from all the walking and running from the

Germans. His holy medal tapped against his chest and clanged against his dog tags, reminding him of the presence of Christ, even in the midst of such hellacious conditions.

"*Ave Maria, gratia plena,*" Messiaen prayed to the Virgin Mary, "*Dominus tecum….sancta Maria, Mater Dei, ora pro nobis peccatoribus, nunc, et in hora mortis nostrae. Amen.* Pray for us sinners now and at the hour of our death. Amen."

He felt as if death would be preferred, yet he was not so foolish as to pray for death. He had much to live for: his wife, his son, his music, and his God.

*****

Chapter 6

Retreat

14 May 1940

The British and French air force bombed the pontoon bridges across the Meuse River, but it was too late. Germany ruled the air and had command of the ground war with their Panzer divisions, mechanical monsters devouring all in their path with their cannons and treading over whatever remained.

At Dunkirk the British and French forces had abandoned their weapons and withdrawn. The Nazi flag flew high over France. Was Paris to be forever consigned to the flames of hell and live under the Sign of the Swastika? The word spread that the Battle for Britain was about to begin.

As an orderly, Messiaen went to work. With an eye to the air, he sought water, food, and shelter for the wounded. He even stitched wounds, his hands and fingers nimble enough from playing the piano and organ. He buried three of the dead and marked their graves with a cross of sticks held together with twine and tapped into the ground with a shovel.

Every morning the air raid sirens sounded and the Stukas came at dawn. What a wake-up call! Then Messiaen and the others would raid cellars for food and wine, stale bread, and soft cheese, among the debris, rubble and mutilated bodies. Even as the destruction and wanton murder continued as the Panzer tank divisions closed in upon the troops, more and more French civilians emerged and cried for help. Messiaen prayed. This was his duty not only as a Christian but as a human being.

The barking dogs of the Nazi soldiers were now less than a few hundred meters away. The burnt-out cars, trucks, busses, and overturned horse-drawn and mule-drawn carts, full of valises, suitcases, clothes, and furniture lined the roads; hundreds of innocent civilians, collateral casualties of the Nazi aggression, formed a parade of refugees. Crying babies, straggling children – some carried by their mothers and fathers or brothers and sisters – were easy targets for the Stukas and Messerschmitts of the Luftwaffe and Panzer divisions of the Wehrmacht.

The scent of oil and petro, burnt homes, spent artillery shells, explosives, and the reeking malodor of death, filled the heavy humid air as hundreds of soldiers and a stream of pilgrims seeking solace in the midst of a war-ravaged countryside trudged along the road between Metz and Nancy.

One never knew when or where the bombs were going to drop, the sounds of exploding ammunition growing closer and closer. The constant barrage of cannon fire and grinding tank treads; the pop-pop-pop of guns and grenades; whistle, thud, boom, whistle, thud, boom of bombs; and the rat-a-tat-tat of machine gun-fire bludgeoned one into living life on the edge. The incoming bombs continued: flashes of light, shells exploding, thunderous echoes and a thick haze of sulfurous air.

A bomb whistled down and landed near Messiaen, the blast threw him to the ground. He sought refuge and crawled through thorn bushes which pierced his flesh. The smell of wild roses and lilac temporarily displaced the stench of war.

Messiaen prayed from the *Imitation of Christ*: *O quam cito transit gloria mundi*. O how quickly passes away the glory of the world. For the German blitz had murdered the youth of spring.

The repeated cacophony resounded in his mind and contributed to a musical idea.

Now that all of France knew that there was indeed open war with Germany, Messiaen knew that Claire must have been beside herself not knowing whether he was alive. As for himself, he wasn't sure whether he would survive the next wave of German attacks.

Will I return? Messiaen asked himself. *Will Pascal have a father? What is Claire left to do all day?* The time moved so slowly for Messiaen, yet how slow each day must move for Claire, how tedious each minute, how mind-numbing each hour, as she wondered what was happening to him. What madness war causes. His fear was whether she and Pascal would remain out of harm's way and safe from the Germans.

His thoughts of Claire and Pascal were quickly displaced by the immediate concern at hand: the need to survive.

There were millions of French refugees on the move. The air raid sirens continued to warn the French of the German attacks. The bodies of women, children, and men lay about in the mud, their valises and personal affects strewn about them.

Messiaen and the other soldiers were hungry, thirsty, wounded, and soaked with sweat and blood, as their blistered toes and heels bloodied their boots. Messiaen ate the last of his bread and memories of a far better France flooded his heart as emotion wept from him.

One more Stuka raid brought a rattling hailstorm of machine-gun fire. Ahead he saw a Church, its spire toppled and roof burning. All of the efforts of the French troops did nothing to halt the advance of the German war machine.

Finally the assault ended and Messiaen collapsed from hunger, exhaustion, and trauma in a ditch with his musical companions.

20 June 1940

Olivier Messiaen, Etienne Pasquier, and Henri Akoka found refuge in a partially bombed apartment building. There was no electricity or running water, but it served its purpose. They hadn't had a solid meal in four days. As they hid in the building they were careful not to attract any attention from the Germans or some of the pro-Nazi French. However, a lone German soldier patrolling the area on his motorcycle somehow spotted them late that evening. They immediately fled the building. Messiaen found a bicycle and placed his haversack of music and scriptures in the basket and pedaled as Pasquier and Akoka ran alongside him. They made their way to a wooded area, but a truck full of Germans followed them with spotlights and soon the Germans' dogs were barking and chasing after them into the woods. Messiaen abandoned the bicycle in a ditch and fled.

"Mon Dieu! How are we ever going to get out of this?" Messiaen cried out as he ran.

"We surrender," Pasquier replied, still running.

"Surrender?" Akoka asked, running faster.

"Do you have any other options?" Pasquier asked harshly.

"No, but I refuse to surrender," Akoka kept his pace, "I know what the Germans do to Jews."

"And I know what the Germans do with those who don't cooperate," Pasquier told Akoka. "Death."

"It's their answer to just about everything," Akoka harrumphed.

"*Death comes for us all*," Messiaen exhaled the words, more like a prayer.

"Not today if we can help it," Pasquier said, slowing to a stop, catching his breath as bent over, placing his hands on his knees.

"Okay," Akoka replied to Pasquier, seemingly ignoring Messiaen's words. "I will surrender— just this once. But I promise to escape."

"You do that," Pasquier said, straightening up.

Messiaen and Akoka stopped and stood next to Pasquier. Messiaen removed his white handkerchief from his pants' pocket and raised it on Pasquier's rifle's bayonet. The German soldiers followed them into the woods with hand torches and surrounded them with machine guns. Messiaen had already dropped his rifle. The Germans approached. One of them spoke French. "*Raus! Raus!* Out, Out! *Lassen Sie Ihre Waffen fallen! Stellen Sie Ihre Hände auf Ihre Helme!* Drop your weapons! Hands on your helmets!"

Another one yelled in German, "*Kommt her! Macht schnell!*" One of the Germans persisted in yelling at Akoka to drop his weapon. He explained to the Germans that it was a clarinet. The Germans laughed and let him keep it.

It was the oddest thing. Here was the enemy up close, but they were just as human as they were and they seemed just as tired. The German soldiers weren't rough with them at all as they led the three Frenchmen out of the woods and to the road.

There was a certain relief in surrendering, even if there was regret that they were surrendering: they were alive, they had survived. They felt dejected that in some way they were letting their country down, their cause was now three men weaker, but since they were now prisoners of war, they would likely wait out the war and go home alive, unlike the dead. Of course, nothing was certain as long as the war raged on. Prisoners of war did not always make it back home. There were too many variables, such as sadistic guards, failed escape attempts, or even becoming a casualty from one's own army attacks. They may have survived this battle, but they weren't in the clear by any means. Yet prisoners of war had their duty to do what they could to sabotage the enemy's plans. But first things first: they had to obey their captors for now.

The three French musicians were forced to march to a German military headquarters where they received a bit of bread and water before being allowed a few hours of rest. The following morning they joined a long line of a thousand French soldiers and were forced to march toward Nancy under an angry sun. Pasquier longed for his cello as Messiaen busied himself jotting down musical ideas, noting especially the song of birds. Akoka occasionally played a melody on his clarinet, helping the other prisoners to get their mind off their predicament.

Incredibly, all the way to the temporary prison camp, French fighters would occasionally engage with German Stukas overhead. The whine of the air raid sirens were part and parcel of everyday life. One German who spoke French told them, "The battle for France is over after 26 years and France has finally fallen."

The Great War was only now at an end, according to Hitler and his henchmen.

Messiaen thought it ironic that his capture nearly coincided with his wedding anniversary of 22 June. "Just in time for my anniversary," he told Pasquier. "My gift to my wife is my survival. *Deo gratias.*"

"The war isn't over," Akoka soberly said as he worked to light a cigarette.

The long march was exhausting and Messiaen's feet were bleeding and he had shin splints. Etienne Pasquier was having trouble walking and Henri Akoka was helping him along. All three of the men were dehydrated and famished in the blazing heat.

All the way to Toul the devastation was everywhere, whole towns destroyed. Of the French citizenry that had not abandoned their towns, they were like the living dead, despondent and emotionless, and very few made eye contact with the French soldiers marching by under close German guard.

There were fire-gutted tanks, both French and German, overturned trucks and armored cars, and dead French soldiers and dead German soldiers.

Bullets and bombs do not discriminate.

"The future may seem black,
but the flowers are in bloom,
the sun is shining,
and the birds are singing."

- Olivier Messiaen

Chapter 7

Prisoners of War

22 June 1940

It was a valley of death, strewn corpses with tattered clothing: soldiers, civilians, men, women, and children.

The wounded were ravaged and gouged with shrapnel, languishing, waiting for death.

One image in particular haunted Messiaen: a mother cradling her dead child, continually trying to rouse him from the sleep of death.

"The war is over for you men," said an older German solder atop a black stallion. There were several soldiers on horseback accompanying the French soldiers as they marched to their prison camp.

"We've got so many of you Frenchies, we don't know what to do."

"Now we rely upon the Providence of God," Messiaen said, "and the help of the Allies."

"You have no allies. The British have retreated."

Mon Dieu, Kyrie eleison. Dona nobis pacem, Messiaen prayed.

The June weather was at its hottest and men struggled along in the dusty conditions carrying whatever possessions they had prodded on by the guards. Some collapsed from heat exhaustion and were put in covered trucks. The number of German soldiers was high to ensure that none of the men escaped.

After marching 40 miles in two days in what seemed a surreal journey through scenes from the Great War, the men arrived at a makeshift compound at Toul, west of Nancy, nothing more than a farmer's pasture surrounded by double barbed wire and German soldiers and guard dogs. Thousands of their fellow French soldiers were already encamped in the meadow, exposed to the burning heat of the June sun, exhausted, hungry, and dehydrated. The few trees that still stood were shorn of leaves and decimated from the blitzkrieg.

Messiaen's feet were swollen, blistered, bloody, and numb from pain. Were it not for the strength and resolve of Henri Akoka, Etienne Pasquier may have been left for dead; Akoka virtually carried Pasquier the last ten miles of the forced march.

Messiaen and his companions were astounded when they began to realize the large number of French soldiers that were in captivity: over a million. At the Toul camp alone there were over 30,000 French soldiers, caged behind barbed wire and guarded by German machine-gunners. The Lorraine camp left thousands exhausted, exposed, and betrayed. The only good thing they heard was that the city of Nancy had been spared major bombing.

The Germans were shocked at the vast numbers of French soldiers they were now responsible for, having crammed them into the space within a few days time. The Germans undoubtedly now believed they were invincible, so surprised at how quickly France fell.

One German boasted that nearly two million French soldiers had surrendered.

Etienne Pasquier offered Messiaen and Akoka each a cigarette.

"Today is 22 June, my wedding anniversary," Messiaen mused as he took the cigarette and placed it in his mouth. "Think they'll let me place a call to my wife?"

"*Mais oui*, just call the Kommandant over," Akoka laughed, grabbing the cigarette from Pasquier. "I'm sure he'll get right on it."

Pasquier lit Messiaen's cigarette for him; Messiaen took a puff.

"It's also Jeanne d'Arc day," Messiaen chuckled, exhaling smoke. "The patron saint of France. How should we celebrate?"

"*Vive le France!*" Henri Akoka cried loudly; several soldiers turned and cheered.

"You idiot!" Pasquier rapped Akoka over the head with his military beret. "That could get your head smashed in. Keep it down!"

"No amount of physical or mental torture will make me accept defeat," Akoka said as he worked to light his cigarette with a match. "We *will* resist!"

The men observed the German soldiers salute their superior officers with the all-too familiar raised right arm with the loud proclamation, "Heil Hitler" as they clicked their heels together.

There was no latrine and after days of marching through the mud, hay, and heat of June they were hungry and thirsty beyond belief, and filthy from wearing the same clothes for nearly two weeks.

In order to relieve themselves, the men were required to humiliate themselves and squat. Hundreds more, indeed thousands of French soldiers, now prisoners, were pushing in from all sides and every single one had the same hope to relieve himself in peace. Soon the stench of the urine and excrement were intolerable. The wounded languished, and many soldiers were ill with vomiting and diarrhea.

The Germans had set up a temporary headquarters in a French farm house, one of the few buildings that wasn't completely destroyed in the siege. The German soldiers were unloading bread from one of the trucks and ate in full view of the French soldiers behind the barbed wire. The French received neither food nor water.

One of the German officers approached Messiaen and his companions at the fence line; his uniform was askew and unbuttoned. He had a loaf of bread in his left hand and a bottle of red wine in his right.

"Paris has capitulated," the German officer announced to the men, as he bit off a piece of bread in front of them.

The aroma of freshly baked bread and the wine's bouquet tantalized Messiaen's heightened senses after weeks of deprivation; the taste of bread and wine in his mouth and on his tongue.

"*Mon Dieu*," Messiaen said. "Civilization has suffered a great blow."

"Yes, one of the world's lights has been extinguished," Henri Akoka agreed.

"Not if we keep the truth alive in our hearts and minds," Messiaen added.

"The Maginot Line and all its fortification didn't stop us at all. We went around it," the German officer gloated, as he washed the bread down with a swig straight from the wine bottle. "But what did you expect? You French never once took into account that we might bring the war to you." The German turned and returned to his men.

"Can you imagine the goosestep of ten thousand German soldiers in Paris," Akoka snarled, "prancing down the *Champs-Élysées* leading Hitler to the *Arc de Triomphe*. What a sight! What an insult! What an outrage!"

On 25 June 1940, after France had surrendered to Germany, an armistice was signed that allowed German authorities to occupy the northern two-thirds of France from the English Channel and along the Atlantic coast. The truce also guaranteed southern France would be free and Vichy would serve as its capital. The situation seemed such a dichotomy: the same nation that gave birth to *Liberté, égalité, fraternité* was now officially a collaborator with Nazi powers, complete with a puppet government.

But there was resistance.

*****

Messiaen used a lot of his time reading his Bible and the *Imitation of Christ*, but the majority of the time he had his musical notebook in hand, jotting down musical ideas and working on the solo clarinet piece he had first introduced to Akoka.

He longed to write his wife to let her know he was alive, but the Germans were making no such provisions. He could only imagine the anxiety and anguish she was experiencing. He prayed for her and all of France and he occupied the rest of the time with his music.

By week's end, the Germans had begun to transport some of the French soldiers to various prison camps in Germany, but Messiaen, Pasquier, and Akoka and roughly 25,000 other Frenchmen were still stranded.

Messiaen reflected upon his predicament. Here he was, a composer; his music had been heard in France, England and the U.S. before the war. He played the pipe organ at Holy Trinity Church and led worshipers in prayer, but now what was he? He was a prisoner and he wondered whether he'd ever compose or perform again. Would he even survive the war? Had all he worked for and done been vainglory? His self-doubts seemed to confirm his vanity in his present predicament.

He clutched the last photograph of Claire and Pascal that he had received in the post before the battle began. In her letter she said all was well but her forlorn face staring at him from the photograph told another tale. Knowing that she was raising Pascal alone was too much to bear, given all that she had already been through.

He longed to be home.

The next few weeks were miserable, waiting in the burning sun and unbearable heat or the pouring rain for transport to a prison camp. Meantime, Messiaen was ready for Henri to resume practicing the piece he had been writing for him before all hell broke loose. Messiaen presented him with the crumpled sheet music and Pasquier reviewed it.

"Henri Akoka," Messiaen announced, "you will be the first to premiere my new work for solo clarinet."

Henri handed the music to Pasquier. "Here, you will be my music stand."

"*Mais oui*, of course," Pasquier chuckled as he placed his lit cigarette in his mouth and held the music sheet for Akoka who practiced the piece.

Akoka again complained of its difficulty, shaking his head in frustration. "I am never going to get it!"

"*Non, non, ami.* Where is that invincible Trotskyite spirit? You will master it. I have faith in you, faith in Man," Messiaen told him. "You will see."

"Faith in Man?" Pasquier laughed. "You certainly jest, Olivier. Now you are sounding like Henri."

Akoka laughed as well as he began to practice the piece. "What did you finally decide to call it?"

"*Abime des Oiseaux.* Abyss of the Birds," Messiaen said, eyeing a warbler alight on the barbed wire fence.

"What does that mean?" Akoka asked.

"The abyss of misery, this temporal world with all its adversity, and the freedom of the birds, their songs, their flight above it all."

"Whatever you say," Akoka said as he began to practice the solo piece again. "But Etienne, hold the music sheet still; the notes are jumping all over the page."

"They're written that way," Messiaen replied seriously with a straight face.

Pasquier laughed as did Akoka. Messiaen simply smiled at his companions. Several of the other prisoners were not as enthusiastic about the work.

"Knock it off with that noise!" an angry Frenchman yelled out.

"*That* is not noise, my friend," Messiaen asserted. "It is music."

"No, it is not music," the angry voice returned. "It's noise."

"It is not noise; it is music," Henri Akoka argued. "Were it not, I wouldn't be able to play it."

"It is music of the future," Messiaen added.

"Then I long not to live," the angry French soldier replied.

The man's words cut Messiaen to the quick. Either his music was noise or it was genius. Either way, however, he knew that he and his music were misunderstood. His only desire was to write music for the glory of God, and in that task to bring others to Christ. He feared he had failed in both respects. How ironic that of the few who did seem to understand his music was his Jewish companion, Henri Akoka.

*****

Three weeks of the grueling agony of waiting for transport and food had taken its toll on thousands of the prisoners. The stench of urine and excrement and vomit had made many of the men ill. Messiaen was pale, his glasses were scratched and bent, yet he was calm and tender though he and his uniform reeked of sweat and grime. All of the men were starving and thirsty. Pasquier gave him some soup, but he barely sipped it. He was far off, as only Olivier could do, seemingly leaving his physical self and taking his soul elsewhere.

He began to hallucinate that he was back home, eating bread and cheese, enjoying a fine bottle of Burgundy wine with his wife, Claire, and playing with his son, Pascal. Messiaen did not want to complain or draw any unnecessary attention to himself, but he was not well. He was delirious, experiencing hallucinations, and felt feverish. However, when he began to pass diarrhea he could no longer hide his illness.

After a few days of illness, he was so dizzy and parched that he no longer had to urinate or defecate since he hadn't eaten or drank in a week. Unable to even rise from the ground, he rolled over into the earth muddied with rain, urine, and excrement.

He was with Claire. She was playing the violin and he the piano. Then he was playing with Pascal. Next he found himself back at Sainte Trinité providing music for the faithful at worship.

He thought of his mother, wondering if she ever foresaw him meeting the fate of a defeated soldier in a conquered France.

In his illness-induced reverie, he clutched tightly to his ramshackle haversack, his rough substitute for his attaché case. Inside were his prized collection of musical scores, prayer books, and scribbling of musical ideas and notations, his only possessions in the world save the worthless raggedy clothes on his back. A recurring nightmare was his music being taken from him by a Nazi guard only to be destroyed.

As Messiaen wavered from lucid consciousness to hallucinations, one of the captured men could no longer bear the anxiety and made a run for the fence. He was halfway through the barbed wire when the soldiers called out "Halt! Halt!" The crazed Frenchman didn't stop or turn around. After another warning, machine gun fire rang out and he went limp on the wires before collapsing to the ground. One of the meanest Germans took the opportunity to remind everyone that the same fate awaited anyone else who had the foolish idea of trying to escape.

Henri Akoka assured them that there were far better methods of escape which were not so obvious. A few of the men bet that he couldn't escape; Henri met their wager in cigarettes. He lit up a cigarette and smoked it as if he were already free.

The Germans had finally secured tents to shelter the men from the elements. The tents housed about 400 men each. However, there still was no fresh water or food. The sound of regular rail service had returned and no doubt some of the trains heard whistling were en route to transport captured French soldiers to awaiting prison camps.

One of the French farm families that refused to leave their house came to the fence one day and offered fresh baked bread, cheese, water, and wine to the men. Unfortunately, it became an ugly scene as the Frenchmen fought each other for what little they could get. Pasquier managed to get a morsel of bread and some water for Messiaen. He brought it back to him and it revived him for a while.

The farmer also gave the men a message from Paris. The Swastika was unfurled over France, and Hitler and the Nazi army had marched triumphantly through the streets of Paris, from the *Place de la Concorde* down the *Champs Elysées* to the *Arc de Triomphe*. But the German propaganda that the Germans were hailed as heroes in Paris was largely orchestrated. The Germans had placed a curfew on Paris and there was growing French resistance through all of France.

Henri Akoka was particularly troubled with the news that the Vichy government had banned all Jewish authors and Jewish professors. There were also credible rumors that French Jews were being rounded up and being relocated in work camps.

Messiaen longed for the happy days of Grenoble and the love of his wife and son.

*****

Chapter 8

Infirmity

10 July 1940

The conditions in the temporary camp were horrid and Messiaen was very ill with dysentery, as were other men. Large numbers of cattle trucks arrived at the gates to the camp that morning to transport the French prisoners to their more permanent prison camps. The men were crammed onto cattle trucks, forty or fifty to a truck, and driven to Nancy. Messiaen felt as if he could go no further.

When they arrived in Nancy they were marched past the train depot and walked to the rail yards where they were herded onto cattle cars commandeered by the German military. Seventy or more prisoners with gear and kit bags were packed into the cars, making it impossible for everyone to lie down or sit down at once, so the men took turns sitting and standing. Messiaen meanwhile drifted in and out of consciousness.

Once the sliding doors of the rail car were closed and bolted, the prisoners had two small openings in the sides of the car for air and light. There was no provision for latrines and the only water they had was whatever they had brought with them. The men had never received the longed-for Red Cross food, and in the horrendous heat the men drank the water from their canteens in the first few hours of the trip.

From the moment the men were locked inside the car, they looked about for ways out of it. Henri climbed atop Pasquier's shoulders to examine the roof of the car looking for a way to escape before arriving at the prison camp, but the Germans had boarded up the openings near the roof to prevent such escapes.

Messiaen, suffering from fever and stomach cramps, languished, wavering in and out of consciousness. The moan of the locomotive echoed off the buildings and through the woods, while the clickety-clack of the rails beneath the rolling wheels of the cars gave Messiaen's musical mind an idea. He noted how the tempo, beat, and measure were irregular and bore no signature time, yet it was a music all its own, not unlike the freedom he had enjoyed before the strident rhythmic symmetry of war, the freedom with which he had composed the clarinet solo piece for Henri Akoka.

The Germans seemingly entertained themselves with the cruel hoax of stopping the train in switchyards for a few hours and leaving the men inside the cars, refusing to let them out to stretch their legs, relieve their bladders, replenish their water supply, scrounge food, or simply breathe fresh air. The train would depart the stops without any efforts made to relieve the men of their squalid conditions; the men like livestock on the way to slaughter.

Some of them sat while the others stood. They could only see out of the cars through the cracks between the boards. The men would squeeze around each other and take turns sitting and standing. Since the men were never let out of their rail cars, they had to relieve themselves in a corner of the car. Messiaen was very ill by this time. He went in and out of consciousness in the rail yards at Dresden where they sat for nearly a day. The heat was insufferable. Many men passed out from heat exhaustion.

By the third day Messiaen was delirious with dehydration and stomach cramps as the dysentery grew worse. He was passing bloody diarrhea, but it was more a bloody mucus; he had a high fever, chills, intense stomach pain, and was wasting away from a loss of weight. Continually cramping, he continually tried to evacuate his bowels. Pasquier and Akoka sought to comfort him as best they could.

By the fourth day enclosed in the cattle car, Messiaen grew worse surrounded by urine and excrement. He was violently ill with fever and hallucinations. Barely conscious at times, he tried to pray, but his mind swirled with sounds and colors as he cast himself upon the mercy of God.

"Seventy men in a filthy cattle car secured with padlocks!" Henri Akoka thundered. "We've been stuck in here for four wretched days going east! Where in hell are they taking us? Russia? *Mon Dieu!*"

"He's right," said one of the young prisoners sitting against the wall of the car. "They're going to kill us."

"Don't be so dramatic," Pasquier said as he turned to his junior. "If they were going to kill us, they would have already done so."

"No, they're taking us deep into *das Vaterland* to kill us slowly and painfully," Henri said, "like good Nazis."

"Keep faith," Messiaen exhorted them in a rare cogent moment. "The Lord will provide...."

Neither man replied, each keeping his personal theological reflection to himself.

When the train came to a stop on the evening of the fourth day, the German soldiers came down the line of cars and unlocked each one. The Frenchmen squinted in the bright sun as they emerged from the squalor. They found themselves in Silesia, in far eastern Germany near the border of occupied Poland, nearly 90 kilometers east of Dresden.

"What city is this?" Pasquier asked.

"Görlitz," one of the Germans answered. "Your new home."

Messiaen was dehydrated, malnourished, and emaciated, surrounded by urine and feces in the rail car; he had had nothing to eat in a week.

"The Red Cross is going to hear about this!" Henri Akoka announced to his captors as he and Pasquier lowered Messiaen out of the cattle car. "Look at the man!"

Messiaen attempted to stand on his own, but he fell into Pasquier's arms.

"If you Frenchies wouldn't have all surrendered like you did, we wouldn't be so overcrowded," the German Kommandant laughed. "We didn't expect to have to feed and house every damned Frenchman 18 to 45. The war is over. Paris is ours."

"If the war is over," Henri asserted, "then just let us go free."

"You Frenchmen are very funny," the German Kommandant replied. "Now get back in line and shut up or you will be going home – in a coffin."

The whites of Messiaen's eyes were yellowish and he could not stand on his own but he clutched his haversack close to his chest. Pasquier helped Olivier Messiaen to one of the passenger benches at the station.

One of the Red Cross volunteers assisted Messiaen onto a medic stretcher as Henri Akoka looked on.

"*Merci, merci beaucoup*, Etienne, Henri...don't worry about me," he said, raspy-voiced, his eyes barely open. "I have united my sufferings to those of Christ. The more a man dies, the more he begins to live for God."

"Oli, I don't know whether to congratulate you or not," Akoka said. "You get to go to hospital while we go to prison."

"*Oui*, the Lord is taking care of me," Messiaen smiled despite the pain that was written across his face and the harrowing pain in his stomach and bowels.

"If that's the case, I'm glad I'm an agnostic," Pasquier laughed.

"You are not an agnostic. You just think you are," Messiaen said as he coughed. "This is my cross..." He tried to say something else, but it all came out as incoherent babbling.

"Don't you die on us, Oli!" Akoka leaned over the stretcher. "It would be a tragedy to have you survive the German blitzkrieg but die of diarrhea."

"I'll be fine," Messiaen said with a slight smile, looking to a nearby tree. "The birds are singing." With that he collapsed on the stretcher and all went black, no longer able to hide or deny his suffering and pain.

A German officer oversaw Messiaen as he was placed in the ambulance. Messiaen was taken to a hospital designated as the prisoner of war hospital in Görlitz and cared for by Polish nuns. The doctor who was caring for him spoke with him and one of the nuns. The German and Polish phrases danced in his head, feeding his colorful dreams and bizarre deliriums.

"Dysentery...a symptom of a potentially deadly illness," the doctor's words came and went, as he explained the condition. "Bloody diarrhea...highly infectious...poor sanitation...bacteria thrives in water contaminated by human feces...sewage mixes with drinking water...infections spread...dirty hands after making toilet....highly contagious."

His first awareness, once he began to recover, was awakening in his room and searching for his haversack with all of his music. It was on the table opposite his bed. It had survived bombs, rain, and the transport. Then he beheld a crucifix and a picture of the Madonna on the wall above the table. But between the two religious images was a framed photograph of *der Führer*.

When the good sister came in to feed him, he asked her, "Sister, why must I share my room with the mustached madman?"

She knew a little French and pointed to Hitler's picture and shook her head, "*Mal homme*." She pointed down the hall to the Nazi guard assigned to the floor where other wounded or ill prisoners of war were being cared for and she made the sign of the cross. From the look on her face, her words could have been, "The Virgin Mary and Our Lord are greatly offended."

Here was the church organist and devout Catholic face-to-face with German Catholics who had compromised their faith to match their Nazi political ideology. Many of the Catholics had abandoned the true faith and settled for a German form of Christianity where Nazism formed the creed. Such *Deutche Christen* faith bowed to Hitler as if Christ.

Messiaen's treatment consisted of oral rehydration, water mixed with salt and sugar, and bread and potatoes. It took him nearly three weeks before he could eat solid food. His thoughts were mixed with delirium and his prayers were sighs too deep for words. There were times he thought he had died for he felt nothing and his mind seemed blank.

He was too ill to get out of bed and too ill to write his wife. The sights, smells, and sounds of the hospital reminded him of the times Claire had been hospitalized after her miscarriages; his days spent sitting by her bedside, holding her hand, wiping her tears and swallowing his own.

In his incapacitation he felt, perhaps for the first time, the torment Christ must have felt as he hung on the cross and cried out: *My God, My God, why have you abandoned me?*

Messiaen had gleaned enough information from the nurses and orderlies at the hospital to learn that Görlitz was an industrial town in Silesia, Germany.

Alone in his hospital bed, he lay listening to the train whistles, church bells, and bird songs. He also read his Bible. He was drawn to the Book of the Apocalypse and he turned to the tenth chapter of the book. In it was an immense angel crowned with a rainbow, the symbol of all colors, and he placed one foot on land and the other on the sea as he lifted his hand toward heaven and said: *"There shall be no more Time."*

What did it mean?

"But on the day of the seventh Angel's trumpet the mystery of God shall be accomplished."

He prayed for understanding.

Thoughts of his wife and son returned as did most of his memory.

After nearly five weeks of rest and delirium he was finally strong enough to get out of bed and walk around the hospital. Messiaen stood in front of a mirror and was shocked; his face was pale and gaunt. He had lost nearly twenty pounds and his pants were loose around his waist. However, he was informed that he was healthy enough to be sent to the prisoner of war camp: Stalag 8A. One of the physicians had taken time to repair his eyeglasses as best as possible, yet the lenses were still scratched.

The day the doctor released him from medical care a German guard took charge of him and escorted him to the prison camp in an official SS staff car.

Messiaen was well aware that his companions had already been in the camp for over a month, and no doubt they were likely convinced that he was dead. He counted it a miracle that he had survived and that his haversack of music and prayer books were still in his possession.

He also knew that he had to write his wife to let her know he was alive and of his whereabouts.

Nonetheless, he now prepared himself for life in a German Stalag.

*****

"The human being is flesh and consciousness,
body and soul;
his heart is an abyss
which can only be filled by the divine."

- Olivier Messiaen

Chapter 9

Stalag 8A

August 1940

The Nazi staff car bore the red, white, and black Swastika flags on either fender as they stiffly flapped in the warm wind. The car left the city and made its way down a dusty tree-lined road. At the end of the road, Messiaen's eyes caught sight of the stark, gaunt compound surrounded by double rows of barbed wire fencing and ten watchtowers evenly situated along the perimeter of the prison camp. The Nazi flag waved over the compound.

Inside the Main Gate stood two command post huts and a series of barracks. From the gates, the road ran down the middle of the camp. Once the car was admitted through the security zone, the Nazi driver stopped the car, got out, and opened the door for Messiaen to get out.

The Kommandant of the camp – an older rotund man – came out of his quarters, gave the Hitler salute, and exchanged a few words with the officer before escorting Messiaen to the processing barrack.

Messiaen took note of the blue frock coats of the prison guards; the blue-grey of the Kommandant and the green grey and blue of the soldiers and guards. Fully armed guards wore blue and black and all the guards carried a rifle on their back. Some were also armed with revolvers and automatic pistols.

Messiaen, still weak, clutched his haversack close. All the barbed wire, 10 or 15 foot tall fences, guard towers, searchlights, flood lamps, and gravel revealed a harsh, barren reality that rendered Messiaen nauseous. He looked around and saw maimed prisoners: patched eyes, bandaged arms, a one-legged man hobbling on crutches, and a one-armed man staring into oblivion.

"Welcome, Frenchies," the Kommandant announced to Messiaen and the dozen other newcomers. "I am Kommandant Colonel Bielas." He kicked up clouds of dirt as he strutted in front of the dozen new prisoners. "I am a veteran of the Great War," Bielas addressed the men. "I survived Verdun in 1916. Four long years we battled you French and we lost the battle, but today I can tell you that we finally won the war after only five weeks of battle." Bielas's chubby face was clean shaven – even missing his eyebrows – but his ears were large and the earlobes hairy.

"For you the war is over," Bielas continued. "This is your new home. Make the most of it. Don't think of trying to escape. Anyone attempting an escape will be shot. The warning wire is your warning. Cross it and you'll be shot. If you are awakened in the middle of the night by gunfire, it's likely that one of your comrades thought he could escape under cover of the night. Don't push your luck. And thank God you were born French."

"And I am your superior officer, men," announced one of the French military officers who was sucking on a Meerschaum pipe. "I am Lieutenant Simon Busseron." Busseron was around 35 years of age, five and a half feet tall, with an aquiline nose and small brown eyes. He made a few introductions and explained a few things about the camp.

"Bielas is the best damned Kommandant we have at Stalag 8A," Lieutenant Busseron said, matter-of-factly, in French.

"He's the only damned Kommandant," one of the French soldiers whispered to Messiaen.

Messiaen nodded while the other men chortled.

Kommandant Bielas nodded to a fierce looking, muscular German with a sub-machine gun. "Lieutenant Schmitt, here, will see that you gentlemen are made presentable for our Stalag."

Lieutenant Schmitt approached Messiaen and the other men to escort them to the disinfestation block. Schmitt's deep-set eyes were shadowed by thick eyebrows; his sideburns came down the side of his face to points near his cheek bones; and his under bite revealed discolored, yellow teeth.

"You gentlemen stink and have lice," the low, husky voice of the stony-faced Schmitt sounded forth. "You need baths and new clothes. You will surrender all your clothes and personal belongings."

"I just came from the hospital," Messiaen tried to reason with Schmitt. "I doubt that I have lice."

"We make the rules here, not you," Schmitt barked. "Get back in line!" The German's breath matched his discolored teeth.

Messiaen clutched his haversack even closer; nothing could make him give it up.

Lieutenant Schmitt stepped close and commanded, "Clothes off!" His pasty tongue licked his top lip as it jutted between his teeth.

"I just came from hospital–" Messiaen attempted to explain.

"Kommandant's orders! Clothes off! And hand over your kit."

"*Non, non, monsieur*," Messiaen held his haversack to his chest. "I beg you –"

"Hand it over!" Schmitt's breath reeked of onions and nicotine as saliva sprayed from his mouth.

"No. Never." Messiaen stared at the German. "Within this kit is contained my treasures –"

"I don't give a good goddamn if you have the holy grail in that kit! Give it to me or I'll shoot," Schmitt threatened.

"Lieutenant Schmitt," Kommandant Bielas called out. "That's enough! He is a composer."

The German soldier lowered his machine gun.

"These orchestral scores are musical treasures that will grant me consolation and solace in the coming months," Messiaen said. "Mark my word, my dear man, your fellow Germans may one day thank you sparing me the misery of having to part with my music. I even have Bach's Brandenburg Concertos along with Debussy's *L'Après-midi d'un faune*, and Stravinky's *Petrushka*."

"You know, normally I would have knocked your head in and then shot you," Lieutenant Schmitt said, "but I like your chutzpah. Men have died for less offense, Frenchie. Yet I will let you live."

Along with the other men Messiaen stripped off his clothes and stood naked like the other prisoners, but he clutched tightly to his haversack.

"Naked as the day you were born and yet he wants to keep his music," Schmitt laughed as he pointed his weapon at Messiaen. "Well, go ahead. Why not? You survived Verdun. Perhaps you will survive the

Stalag." The German laughed at the lanky bespectacled Messiaen and announced to all: "He's a harmless dreamer. He'd rather have his music than his clothes!" Schmitt then again aimed the gun at Messiaen with the command, "Go!"

Messiaen and the other naked men were escorted into the disinfestation block and sprayed down receiving all the dignity of stray dogs being dipped for fleas.

Messiaen was assigned the number 35333.

In the 1930s Stalag 8A was initially a *Hitlerjugend* (Hitler Youth) camp, but when the war began the camp buildings came under control of the *Wehrmacht* and became the prisoner of war camp *Stammlager* VIIIA, otherwise known as Stalag 8A. By October 1939 it was home to more than 15,000 Polish soldiers taken prisoner during September of 1939.

After a tour of the camp, Messiaen was assigned to Barracks 19A where Akoka and Pasquier were assigned. The two men were astounded when they saw the tall, gaunt figure of Messiaen appear.

"Can it be? Are you a French ghost?" Henri Akoka gasped upon seeing Messiaen approach.

"*Mon Dieu!* He's alive!" Etienne Pasquier exclaimed incredulously as he hurried to greet him. "We'll have to call you Lazarus!"

"I'm not that easy to kill off," Messiaen said as he embraced Akoka.

"We had given up all hope and imagined your body already in the ground," Pasquier said before he kissed Messiaen on both cheeks.

"Divine Providence has spared me," Messiaen said, raising his eyes to the heavens as he crossed himself. "The Lord still has work for me to do here." It was the first time he had smiled in several weeks.

"How did you manage to keep your haversack?" Pasquier asked. "You could have lost all of your music."

"My life is God's. And the music was never mine to begin with. Possession is such an illusion. All is gift; everything is a gift from the hand of God."

"We already have two chaplains, professor Messiaen," Lieutenant Busseron interrupted. "We'll simply call you 'our Mozart of the Stalag'."

Either by Divine Providence or German order, the musicians would have the good fortune of each others' company. That small blessing would have to suffice as they bore the desolation of incarceration.

*****

Messiaen became familiar with the Stalag 8A. There were French, Belgian, British, and Polish soldiers being held and the number of prisoners increased daily for the first few weeks, brought in by truck and train.

The camp was in disrepair, with broken windows and doors, and a shortage of beds. What beds they had were cheap paillasses, thin mattresses filled with straw and sawdust. The camp was infested with lice and bedbugs.

As the influx of French and Belgian prisoners increased, nearly 30,000 prisoners were sent there – the majority French, even though the facilities were originally intended for 15,000. The Red Cross could not provide enough food rations. However, most of the prisoners were living in commandos, camp annexes where the men were sent as workers on farms, mines, and factories. Even though most of the Polish and French prisoners had been employed as laborers, there was still severe overcrowding. Many of the prisoners – Polish, Czechoslovakian, French, and Belgian – were living in tents; the remaining Polish prisoners were employed building barracks. Overall about 3000 prisoners of war were in the camp any given day.

There were two barracks for camp officials, latrines, the infirmary, two kitchens, a canteen, a barracks of showers, a barracks for mail, one as a theatre, another as a chapel and camp library. There was a further hut used as a jail, surrounded by a fence, usually used for putting certain prisoners in solitary confinement.

There were about another 30 barracks for the prisoners, 15 on either side of the road that divided the camp. The barracks measured 50 by 10 meters with only one door at the front. The bunks were three-tiered and each barracks held about 350 men. In the middle of each building was a stove and two washrooms. The men themselves were allowed hot showers twice per week. Outside the barracks were two toilet rooms. All the waste water flowed into trenches that led away from the camp. The stench of the latrines was deplorable and even their drinking water was tainted because of the odious sewer that ran so close to the camp water supply. The prisoners opened the windows in the summer, but the smell of sewage from the ditch made the air loathsome.

For recreation, the French and Belgians cleared a swath of ground for a soccer field. Many of the prisoners played ball as the guards looked on with vigilant eyes and ready rifles.

After evening roll call that first night, Messiaen made his way to his bunk and dusted his mattress off, sneezing at the dust and smell of sawdust and straw.

"Barrack 19A's best," Henri Akoka laughed as he came up to Messiaen.

Messiaen's spot was on the lowest bunk opposite Henri Akoka. The spot above Henri was empty.

"Whose bunk is that?" Messiaen asked Akoka.

"Poor chap tried to escape as soon as he got here," Akoka explained, glancing away. "The only good thing is he didn't suffer long. They gunned him down on the wires."

Messiaen said nothing but prayed for the man. As he readied for bed, he wrote his wife, Claire, well aware that she too had likely given him up for dead. He could only imagine her anguish and the toll the madness of the war had taken upon her already delicate condition.

19 August 1940

Ma Mi Chérie,

For the last month I have been a prisoner in Germany and I am sending you my first letter today. Please be assured that I am indeed alive. Reply to me at the following address: Messiaen, Olivier, prisoner no. 35333, Stalag VIIIA, Germany.

Are you well? How is Pascal? I am well. I was captured 20 June, but due to illness I contracted while imprisoned I am only now able to write. I have a kit-bag, my miniature scores, and some underwear. Could you send me a parcel containing: a razor, a shaving brush, razor blades, shaving soap, shoelaces, a new kit-bag, a sweater (a large one!), a pair of socks, a handkerchief, chocolate, sugar, cake, and gingerbread?

Embrace for me my father and brother. Give my news to Abbé Hemmer and to Marcel Dupré so that I can get back to my posts as organist, and as a professor of harmony at the Paris Conservatoire. Every day I pray for Pascal and for you, and ask for all of us to be granted patience, a gift of the Holy Spirit. I long for my home, my music, and above all for your sweet presence, and I embrace you with all my heart! I hope this note arrives quite quickly so as to calm your worries! Caress my little Pascal's fair hair, and a huge kiss for my Mi whom I love.

Olivier

*****

He worried about what Claire thought. How many days had she considered him dead? A war-widow with a fatherless son. MIA. POW. Who knows how this will end?

Yet Messiaen believed with all his heart that though evil flourished, the mystery of God would be revealed. Wickedness and evil seemed to hold sway, but in the end, God would conquer evil, good would win over evil. Whether in this life or the next, there would be the triumph of good where all questions would be answered and all wrongs would be righted! Such was his prayer.

He sealed the letter and put it in the out-going mail.

At 21:00 hours, the guards blew a whistle and ordered the men to barracks. Messiaen observed his fellow prisoners filing in the barracks. For the next hour he read his *Imitation of Christ*, said his evening prayers, and pondered the musical score of Stravinky's *Petrouchka*.

At 22:00 hours he was startled as the guards blew another whistle and all went black: lights out. The men raised a collective moan of lament; Messiaen tucked his book and notes inside his well-worn haversack and lay in the darkness trying to ignore his hunger pains.

The bark of locomotives, their clanging bells, and the asthmatic wheeze of the whistles was a constant reminder he was going nowhere. He tossed and turned but sleep eluded him. His mind was darting to and fro, from Claire, to Pascal, to the war, to food; from the memory of his mother, to music, the organ, the piano, birds, a musical idea, and back to God.

*****

Chapter 10

Prison Life

A rapping percussion sounded in Messiaen's ears, but he dismissed it as a bad dream where all the sights and sounds blended into something incomprehensible. Finally he realized it was not a dream, but was a German guard pounding on the doors of the barrack.

"Olivier! Wake up! Roll call!" Henri Akoka's dusky face loomed large, hovering above Messiaen as he shook the composer as he lay in his bunk.

"What?" Messiaen squinted in the sunlight.

"Rise and shine! Our neighbors, the friendly Germans want to count us! They have nothing better to do."

"*Mon Dieu!* What time is it?"

"6:30!"

"I did not sleep well last night," Messiaen lamented.

"Who does? Count your blessings. They let us sleep in today."

"Did they now?" Messiaen asked. "Well, that was awfully kind, given the circumstances and the fact that there's a war on."

"*Oui,*" Akoka replied with a sigh.

The two men buttoned their uniforms, put on their shoes, donned their military berets and stepped out into the cool, crisp morning air. Messiaen heard a nightingale singing and caught sight of it flitting along the barbed wire as piercing rays of sunlight filtered through traces of fog.

The men stood at attention as the German officer read through each name.

"How often do we do this?" Messiaen whispered to Akoka who was standing just to his left.

"Every morning. Sometimes twice, morning and evening."

"Lovely," Messiaen sniggered.

"No, what's loveliest of all is roll call in the middle of the night after someone tunnels out. The SS come in with their dogs, search all the barracks, and pick a few of us to shake down and interrogate. You don't forget those moments."

One of the officers shouted at Akoka for talking and their conversation was at an end.

Following roll call, the men were allowed to go to the canteen to receive half a liter of hot water per man for making tea or coffee or for washing clothes. Their breakfast consisted of a slice of black bread, though it was mostly a mix of sawdust and flour. Messiaen held the ersatz bread in his hand and took note of the wood shavings in the bread.

"You'll get used to the bread," Henri laughed. "If you eat enough of it, you'll turn into Pinocchio."

"Watch for splinters in your bread, gentlemen," one of the French cooks said, observing some new prisoners in the breakfast line.

"Splinters?!" an angry Frenchman exclaimed and cursed.

"Weevils and roaches are considered protein," the Frenchman announced.

"They're also extra," Akoka laughed.

After breakfast – or the lack thereof – Messiaen found his way to the chapel at Barracks 28A. One of the French prisoners was an artist who had painted several religious works, including a picture of the Lord's Supper above the High Altar.

The priest assigned to the French Catholics in Messiaen's section of the camp was Abbé Jean Brossard, a military chaplain captured at Verdun. He provided the Sacraments to the men, both captors and prisoners. Abbé Brossard was about the same age as Messiaen. In his black soutane, his long face and tired hazel eyes revealed battle fatigue. He wore his thinning black hair short and parted on the left. Messiaen spoke with Abbé Brossard who informed him that Mass was celebrated after roll call, before breakfast. The priest also informed him that Hut 27B had been transformed into a theatre while 28B was a lecture hall.

For the most part, the prisoners were free to do as they wished during the day. This was some comfort for Messiaen the composer, who knew that in order to retain his sanity he would have to work at his composition daily.

*****

There were still not enough food supplies owing to the huge numbers of French soldiers taken as prisoners, and the Red Cross packages had yet to arrive, so the men were allowed only one bowl of soup per day.

Etienne Pasquier lived in the barracks with the cooks; 40 prisoners worked in the kitchen to feed the 3000 or more men. Between 10 a.m. and 2 p.m. the soup was served. Henri Akoka described the sole meal of the day as a mysterious stew of sorts. The men called it *Piss Soup*, a "urinary delight," mainly consisting of a weak watered broth with very few potatoes, cabbage and turnips: very distasteful and unfulfilling, a slop of a stew.

"Bon appétit!" a surly German soldier laughed as two French cooks carried in the large tub of boiling water.

"It smells like water from the dirty laundry," Messiaen sneered.

"It is! It is!" Akoka exclaimed to his fellow prisoners.

The German guards laughed as Pasquier ladled some of it out to those first in line.

"Did the Brits make this stew?" Henri Akoka asked. "Where's all that splendid German food we hear about?"

"Shut up and eat," the German guard shouted.

"If you find a mouse in your soup," Pasquier announced as he dipped the ladle back on the pot, "don't say anything or else every other man in the camp will want one."

"Can we at least have horsemeat?" Henri Akoka joked.

"All we have is rat," Pasquier winked to his two musical compatriots.

"What are they doing to us?" Messiaen chuckled. "Why are they starving us? In the hospital they fed me very well. Did they only nurse me back to health in order to starve me to death?"

"*Oui*," Akoka laughed. "Exactly."

"If so, then these Germans have a wonderfully morbid sense of humor. '*You have to be healthy before we can kill you*'," he said adopting a German accent.

"Olivier, you make me laugh," Akoka said, putting his arm around Messiaen. "But the Nazis are morbid and they do intend to starve us to death."

Messiaen, for his part, sat and said a prayer of blessing before he ate his soup.

"You are a dear man," Akoka smiled. "Most men utter a curse over this pitiful soup; but you still find it within your heart to give thanks. You are an enigma, my friend. An enigma. Simply a mystery," Akoka said. "An avant-garde composer who is a devoutly religious man."

"God is a mystery," Messiaen mused, "and we are His children."

"*Oui*," Akoka replied. "This is true. Men of God are a mystery. And you are His child."

Again, Messiaen felt misunderstood. Sometimes he even felt as if his fellow musicians were patronizing him.

*****

Over the course of a week, Messiaen had learned much from the imprisoned soldiers. Some men working in the commandos were able to bribe the guards for info. There was also a radio somewhere in the camp and the men were listening to the BBC. The German *Luftwaffe* was attacking Britain in nightly bombing raids of London. The British Prime Minister, Winston Churchill, was vowing that the British Empire, and France, led by General de Gaulle and his gallant band of the Free French Forces and the French Resistance, would conquer Hitler and Nazism, so that France, and all of Europe, would be restored to its full freedom and ancient fame.

By now all of the prisoners – British first, then French – had heard of Churchill's rousing speech where he said: *"Let us therefore brace ourselves to our duty and so bear ourselves that if the British Commonwealth and Empire last for a thousand years, men will still say 'This was their finest hour!'"* Now that the Battle for Britain was being waged, his words inspired the men.

The German-controlled Vichy Police were betraying their own French people. The Gestapo was rounding up French Resistance partisans in Paris and elsewhere, though General de Gaulle's influence continued to gain momentum for the French Resistance. Even so, the Nazis themselves were the best recruiters for the Resistance in occupied France. It was in the free-zone of Vichy-controlled France that the general populace had been lulled to sleep and grown indifferent to the cause of the resistance, becoming collaborators, accepting their fate.

Yet even though Messiaen and the other French tried to make their captivity as bearable as possible, the presence of double barbed-wire fences, searchlights, machine guns, patrols, and guard dogs never let the men forget that they were still imprisoned as their beloved France was being ruled by Nazis. Messiaen's growing fear was that he would never again compose music.

There was also the "survivor guilt" of some of the prisoners. Many had witnessed the deaths of friends and fellow soldiers. There was additional guilt knowing that many of their partisans were being denied basic rights that they were enjoying – letters, books, and cigarettes, not to mention the observers from the Red Cross who made sure they were not abused.

A few soldiers committed suicide when they learned that their families had been killed in either the German attack or in one of the roundups conducted by the Gestapo, the German Secret Police.

"I feel like I am living in a damned tomb!" Henri Akoka exclaimed one evening as the men walked the grounds. They had received bad news from Paris: a group of the French Resistance was discovered and shot. "The damned Nazis with their gleaming smiles, polished boots, shining uniforms, and glistening weapons! Saboteurs we will be! In occupied France the resistance is growing, the British may have fled, but they will be back. Mark my word! If Hitler thinks he can win the war by harassing civilian populations and killing women and children he is sadly mistaken. The will of the French is stronger that this armistice.

"My purpose and goal as a prisoner is to escape," Akoka exclaimed, as he flung the remains of a well-smoked cigarette to the wind. "Who the hell are we trying to fool? I'm busting out of this damned bird cage!"

*****

The Chapel at Stalag 8A

"What comes from the organ is
invisible music, propelled by wind,
yet whose instrument gives no sign of activity,
and whose player normally cannot be seen.
Organ music symbolizes and makes real
the contact between the mundane and the eternal.
Indeed it makes a sacrament of all the world."

- Olivier Messiaen

Chapter 11

The Violin

September 1940

Fall was in the air as the crisp temperatures turned the leaves to gold, red, brown, and violet. Messiaen reflected on the past year since leaving Paris.

The War on Britain continued. What little news they heard from the BBC was not good. Reports were that London was burning. The prisoners had nothing to do and could only learn what was happening through the occasional news from one of the guards or when one of the prisoners got a report from listening in to the wireless which was hidden somewhere in the camp. The prisoners also published a monthly newspaper for the camp, *Le Lumignon* (the Light), although it was censored by the authorities.

The number of German soldiers at the camp increased. They were all members of the German Army. Some of the men were transferred to Görlitz after being wounded in the French offensive; others came from the Battle of Dunkirk. Some of the guards were young men who had been in the *Hitlerjugend*, others were older men, some veterans of the Great War. The rest were civilians who were drafted into service. It seemed that these men were either apathetic or ruthless. If one of the prisoners strayed too close to the warning wire, there was the fear of being shot.

The prisoners learned quickly which guards could be trusted and which ones could not. Some of the prisoners were beginning to push their luck with the German guards by whistling or humming the "*La Marseilles*" in their barracks and around the camp. Henri Akoka entertained himself by playing variations of the tune on his clarinet merely to irritate the guards.

The Germans began to enforce the rule of separation among the Belgians, Poles, Czechoslovakians, Brits, and French. The men were not to speak to the guards, but the rule was lax for French since their government had capitulated and signed the armistice. Some of the guards could be bribed with coffee, chocolate, cigarettes, and jams from the Red Cross parcels.

The French prisoners were growing cold to the Germans. "I heard Paris is burning," Schmitt told the men. "Your *Notre Dame* is nothing but a pile of smoldering sticks and stones." He laughed, his yellow lower teeth scraping his upper lip as his pasty tongue with strands of saliva danced between his teeth and lips.

"Very funny," Henri Akoka replied, "but that's not what your Anti-Allied propaganda papers say."

"And it's certainly not what the BBC is reporting," Jacques Chevalier said; he was a smart-aleck Frenchman with an upturned nose, full head of brown hair, and athletic build.

There was deathly silence.

"It was a joke, Sir," said Jacques Chevalier, but it was too late.

"No more privileges!" Schmitt barked in his husky voice as his eyes blazed.

"What, no film?" Jacques Chevalier asked. "It's Saturday night, Schmitt. Where's your sense of humor?"

"Shut up!" Schmitt pointed his gun at Chevalier, his eyebrows scrunched down over his eyes. "Do you want to invite the Gestapo in here?"

At that Schmitt left the barracks and Chevalier engaged Messiaen in conversation.

"So Professor Messiaen, what do you make of the German's notion of freedom?"

"True freedom has nothing to do with a fantasy of the pure race or desire to do with others as one likes. True freedom is constructive — arrived at through self-control, respect for others, and the search for truth. True freedom is a foretaste of heaven, for Christ said, 'If you live by my word, then you will know the truth, and the truth will set you free.'"

"Well, I have heard your music," Chevalier laughed, "And it betrays the order you claim, the order of this just God of yours, the perfection of heaven. What about the imperfection of the earth? It sure seems disordered to me and to millions of others, especially those of us stuck behind barbed wire."

"That is because we are here on earth and our ears cannot – and do not – hear heaven yet. We long for heaven and that is why we pray for God's kingdom to come here on earth. God is beyond all time – outside of time. Indeed there is no time with God. Christ's Resurrection from the dead is the cause and root of all our hope."

"How can you claim to be a good Catholic – indeed, a Christian – and produce the type of noise you do?" Chevalier asked.

"How can you claim to be a Christian and not understand that the scripture commands us to make a joyful noise unto the Lord?" Messiaen retorted. "It may just be noise to you, but I know that it is music for it brings me great joy. I am giving praise and glory to the Lord through my music."

"It is dissonant noise. You are dissonant. Nothing more," Chevalier huffed.

"It is not dissonant noise and I am not dissonant. Wash your ears out."

Messiaen's retort earned a roar of hoots, howls, and applause as the men threw dirty socks and clothes at Chevalier and told him to pipe down.

*****

That same week, Messiaen, Pasquier, and Akoka were greeted by a newcomer to the prison camp. He was Jean Le Boulaire, a prisoner from another prison camp, but relocated to Stalag 8A in Görlitz. Jean Le Boulaire had a rich resonant voice, full and deep, quite sonorous, vibrant. He was bitter from his war experience, and his sparkling blue eyes held within them a certain sadness. Le Boulaire was beat up: his face was bruised, he walked with a limp, and he still had shards of shrapnel in his back.

Jean Le Boulaire was assigned to the same bunk as the French clarinetist Henri Akoka. Le Boulaire had terrible childhood memories of the Great War. "Many of the men my father's age returned home maimed, disfigured, and emotionally scarred," he said, his eyes cast down. "Many of my school friends were war orphans, having lost their fathers to the war."

Le Boulaire explained to the men that from 1934-36 he had served in the military and was redeployed in 1938 and he had been sent to the Maginot Line in 1940.

"I was at the Battle of Dunkerque from May to June with the British." Jean Le Boulaire described his experience as he bummed a cigarette from Akoka and sat on the bench at the end of the row of bunks. "We were in full retreat when our unit managed to secure a boat and float back to England. We thought for sure that the Luftwaffe would kill us all. Then when we regrouped and rearmed, we sailed back across the channel and landed along the Brittany coast. We were almost to Paris when the Panzers and Luftwaffe clobbered us. We fought hard, but the Germans kept coming. There were thousands of us who finally surrendered when we realized the battle was lost." Le Boulaire stopped speaking at that point, his sonorous voice cracking.

"It's all right, we understand," Messiaen said, placing his right hand on Le Boulaire's left shoulder. Messiaen's own horrible memories of the war vividly returned.

"I've been to hell," Le Boulaire said, shaken and sullen. "The devil wears a swastika and speaks German. I prefer not to speak of what I have seen and participated in. It's too painful."

The men all agreed. Jean Le Boulaire stood and began to arrange his possessions in the small living quarters when he caught sight of Akoka's clarinet.

"Whose clarinet?" Le Boulaire asked as his eyes sparkled with traces of hope.

"It's mine," Akoka replied. "Do you play?"

"I am a violinist," Le Boulaire's eyes brightened slightly, looking up.

"I am a cellist," Pasquier said.

"I play the piano and organ," Messiaen said.

"He's the camp composer," Akoka added, patting Messiaen on the back.

"I lost my violin at Dunkerque," Le Boulaire explained.

"The only instrument we have at the moment is Henri's clarinet."

"Was I removed from the other camp to be sent here to play music?"

"The Lord does provide, *non?*" Messiaen answered.

"Please. No talk of God for me. As far as I am concerned, God is dead. If God was good, then he would certainly never allow for what the Nazis are doing to Europe."

"Yet your righteous indignation attests that God is just," Messiaen smiled.

"God is *just?* Please," Le Boulaire asked him, his brows furrowed. "Are you a priest? I don't like priests. They're pushy."

"*Non, non*, I am a mere church organist; the choir loft is the closest I get to the sanctuary."

"You had me fooled. I was raised Catholic. You look like a priest. Keep your religion to yourself."

"*Father* Messiaen," Pasquier joked. "He is our composer-priest."

"*Olivier* Messiaen?" Le Boulaire straightened up in his chair. "*The* Olivier Messiaen, composer, and member of *Jeune France?*"

"*Oui,*" he answered, lowering his head a bit. "Forgive my appearance. I haven't received any shaving cream."

"*Oui,*" Henri said, "Saint Francis of the Stalag. He preaches to the birds, you know."

"No," Messiaen corrected him, "the birds preach to me."

"I knew of you, and even attended a few of your orchestral performances," Le Boulaire said. "It is curious, though, how the Kommandant seemed to know of my musical career," Le Boulaire continued. "He even knew that I had studied at the Paris Conservatoire. Is that not ironic? My musical talents were never appreciated in Paris, yet the Nazis express an interest in me as a violinist. What a strange world it is in which we live."

War has a way of breaking down men's defenses rather quickly, revealing their vulnerabilities. The uncertainty of prison life — let alone the chaos of war with Germany — left many of the men angry and ashamed as well as relieved. After lights out, Messiaen and Le Boulaire talked late into the night that first night as Henri Akoka fell asleep listening.

"I was raised Catholic," Le Boulaire said, smoking a cigarette in his bunk. "But once I went away to school, I was finished with religion."

"Interesting, isn't it?" Messiaen said, as he ran his finger up and down the wooden beam of his bunk. "My father was a nominal Catholic but my mother was an agnostic at best, so I took it upon myself and embraced Catholicism."

"A priest once told me I was going to hell," said Le Boulaire, inhaling on his smoke, the red glow revealing his face. "Ever since then, I haven't heard Mass."

"One bad priest shouldn't discredit the entire Church," Messiaen said, stopping his hand on the wooden bunk frame.

"Admit it, if the Church were true to her mission, would the pope have signed a concordat with Hitler?" Le Boulaire argued.

"The concordat maintained that clergy were not to engage in political activity, but it also recognized the Church and enabled Catholics to continue to practice their faith."

"Semantics, my friend," Le Boulaire laughed. "Try telling that to the political victims of Hitler and all the Jews of Europe."

"Pope Pius XII has called the dictators of Europe enemies of Christ; Saint Paul wrote that there is neither Gentile nor Jew in Christ."

"I don't want to talk about it. If the pope had seen what I saw, he'd empty the church's coffers to help the refugees and condemn Nazism once and for all!"

"I wish it were all that simple," Messiaen lowered his head as if in prayer. "This I do know: the Lord hears the cry of the poor, the widow, and the orphan. He is close to the broken-hearted and those whose spirit is crushed."

"Yes, well, the Lord might hear and see them, but He's certainly remained inactive to relieve them of their lot."

"That is our task. We must be the Body of Christ."

"Well, whatever you say, old man." Le Boulaire lit another cigarette in his bunk and shook his head at Messiaen. "I just wish I had my violin." Le Boulaire said no more.

Messiaen took his rosary from his shirt pocket and thumbed the beads.

*****

Messiaen considered the clarinet piece he had written for Akoka and began to expand his musical idea into a concept for a quartet of musicians: piano, clarinet, cello, and violin. With Jean Le Boulaire's arrival he now had enough men for a quartet.

"That's a great idea, Olivier," Akoka said one afternoon over his soup of nothing but broth and wood shavings, "but all we have is my clarinet."

"Minor detail," Messiaen replied, drinking his ersatz coffee. "The Lord will provide. He always does."

"Really?" Le Boulaire asked, pushing his bowl aside. "Not to sound blasphemous, but if God can secure for us musical instruments, could you put in a good word so that he can end this war? I'd really like to go home and see this Nazi madman off the world's stage."

"*Oui, oui*, we'd all like that, now wouldn't we?" Messiaen smiled as he sipped his soup off the spoon.

"Yes, but Henri, you keep threatening to escape," Pasquier laughed, "then where would we be?"

"I don't know about the rest of you," Akoka answered, tossing his spoon in his soup bowl, "but I'd be back in Paris working to dismantle this damned Nazi machine."

*****

Over time Messiaen began to learn about the lives and thoughts of some of the German guards. Many of the guards considered their tasks merely as a job. Some were apolitical and indifferent to Nazi ideals, and had been prevented from attending university or their education was interrupted by the war and they were drafted into the German army and sent to the western front. Others among them were soldiers at heart and had been indoctrinated with Nazi ideals from their youth beginning with the *Hitlerjugend* and they were frustrated that the war was over for them.

Messiaen had befriended one of the guards since arriving. This was strictly forbidden, but it seemed every rule was made to break in Stalag 8A. The guard was Hauptmann Karl Albert Brüll, an older guard assigned to Messiaen's barrack. Brüll never raised his voice to the inmates unlike the other guards, and he certainly wasn't an SS man.

Brüll had a receding hair line and he was overall a thin man. His eyes were kind and green, his smile contagious. He was very careful with his words, delicately weighing each one, and he spoke French besides German. Messiaen learned that he was a practicing attorney before being drafted into the German army. He was also a music lover and a Catholic. This was all Messiaen needed to know.

By late September Brüll confided in Messiaen that his mother was Belgian and his father a devout Catholic and president of the Catholic Youth of Silesia.

Brüll respected the prisoners, even the Jews. Messiaen knew that Brüll was a good man, even if he wore the Nazi German insignia. One day, Brüll showed him to one of the rooms of the latrine. It was a room with no windows and a single light bulb suspended from the ceiling. "You can compose here where it is quiet."

"*Merci beaucoup,*" Messiaen acknowledged Brüll. "*Danke Schön.*"

Messiaen slept little and he awoke early and entered the room to compose. He would even sneak there late at night. Meanwhile Brüll brought Messiaen some pencils, erasers, and music paper. He even gave him a few new reeds to give Henri Akoka for his clarinet.

"My parents would take me to the symphony and opera as a child," Brüll explained as he smoked his cigarette down to the end. "I love music: Bach, Mozart, Beethoven, and Brahms."

*****

Dirty and sweaty, Messiaen's clothes reeked. The sound of trucks, barking guard dogs, and train whistles ever reminded him of his predicament. The mattresses of straw, shabby uniforms, and cold draft through the barracks, where he was on the lowest bunk where it was coldest, were privations with which he struggled to endure. He missed his wife, his son, Paris, his church, his organ, his piano, his students, and his birds.

Hauptmann Brüll offered Messiaen bread on several occasions. The first time he sneaked some bread into Messiaen's knapsack was after a morning roll call.

"My wife made it for you," he whispered over his shoulder. "Share some of it with your Jewish friend and the violinist, Le Boulaire."

Though Brüll never said it explicitly, Messiaen deduced enough from their conversations and clandestine meetings that he was more a German nationalist than a Nazi and suspected that Brüll only wore the Nazi Eagle and Swastika as part of his uniform, for his soul betrayed Nazi ideals.

There was in the bread a sweetness. The reality of a German offering him, a defeated Frenchman, a loaf of bread held within it great promise. Messiaen held to the firm belief that the Good God would prevail and deliver them all from the ravages of war.

He wept as he was nourished by the bread of this German angel of mercy, and he recognized as his hand touched his that all men were brothers. Just as the birds outside his window sang praise to God and flew freely wherever they pleased, so were all men intended to be free. All the human lines of demarcation, national and ethnic boundaries, even those divisions written with the blood of the victims of racist, totalitarian regimes would not stand. Messiaen knew with certainty that Christ prepares a celestial banquet for people of all tribes, races, languages, and nations.

One night, Hauptmann Brüll surprised Messiaen by waking him in the early hours of morning. At first he feared it was the Gestapo. Brüll took him outside to behold the northern lights of the aurora borealis. Green, blue, and violet drapes shimmered across the skies. Together the two men stood in awe of the beauty of nature. Was it a sign? Messiaen nodded in appreciation as he returned to his barracks.

The next morning after roll call there appeared a violin on Jean Le Boulaire's bunk.

"Who did this?" Le Boulaire exclaimed with delight at the find.

"It is a miracle. I told you the Lord would provide, *non?*" Messiaen nodded.

Messiaen knew that the Lord had an agent in the camp and that his name was Brüll.

*****

Chapter 12

The Cello

Since Etienne Pasquier was assigned to the kitchen, he sneaked extra portions of potatoes to Messiaen when he could and he pilfered whatever other food he could without being caught. He sold potatoes to some of the other men and even stole bread and sugar and *fromage blanc* from Kommandant Bielas's supplies.

Even though Pasquier was giving extra provisions to Messiaen, Messiaen would in turn give his extra portions to some of the other prisoners, all the while offering up his suffering and privations for his wife and his son.

Yet Messiaen was not well. He had lost even more weight since arriving at Stalag 8A and had fallen unconscious on several occasions, likely still suffering from his bout with dysentery from the time of his capture. He was disoriented, pale, and hallucinating; his hunger pains even gave him hallucinations of color.

One afternoon, Brüll surprised Pasquier in the lunch line, appearing from nowhere. "Pasquier, men have died for less!"

"What are you talking about Hauptmann Brüll?"

"You know what I am talking about: the Kommandant's supplies! The other guards would show you no mercy and shoot you on sight."

Suddenly Lieutenant Erich von Schmitt appeared in the mess hall. "And Pasquier," the voice of the side-burned lieutenant sounded forth. "I'd suggest you find those missing serving spoons and pails. The German cooks are getting suspicious about diggers."

"What's a digger?" Pasquier asked, knowing exactly what he meant.

"Very funny." Schmitt's distorted smile with discolored teeth mismatched his husky voice and muscular build.

Messiaen had heard that in one of the barracks underneath a middle bunk was a false floor that led to a trap door that opened to a tunnel. There were also rumors of men digging night and day. He knew that

Akoka was one of the diggers; the dirt under his fingernails betrayed the fact.

The four musicians, Olivier Messiaen, Henri Akoka, Etienne Pasquier, and Jean Le Boulaire, along with the French Lieutenant Simon Busseron and Sergeant Jacques Chevalier, walked the boundaries of the camp one cold October evening as the grey sky spat an icy mist of rain and sleet.

"Are you on the Escape Committee?" Corporal Pasquier asked Akoka.

"Are we among friends?" Akoka smiled behind his cigarette. "A prisoner is made to escape."

"The guards shot and killed an escapee just last night." Messiaen said as he placed his fingers under his arms, his fingerless gloves failed to keep his fingers warm or prevent them from getting numb from the cold.

"*Oui*. Who didn't hear the machine-gun fire?" Jacques Chevalier asked. "And if that wasn't enough, then the damned Krauts dragged the dead body into the center of the camp for all to see. You'd think they'd bagged an elk."

"Touching, isn't it?" Lieutenant Busseron said, removing his pipe from his mouth. "At least the Germans covered the corpse with a blanket."

"Lucky bastard," Jean Le Boulaire coldly responded, his warm breath briefly appearing in the air. "The war's more than over for him. At least they won't be able to starve him to death."

"I think he let the Germans help him commit suicide," Lieutenant Busseron said as he worked to relight his pipe. "His brother died trying to escape from Stalag Luft III last month. Then he got a letter last week. His wife, son, mother, father, and sister were all killed at Metz during a bombing raid."

"But the Germans aren't all bad, are they Olivier?" Akoka asked Messiaen, turning to him.

"War changes everything," Messiaen muttered, almost absent-mindedly as he stared off into the distance as a song thrush atop the barbed wire chirped a melody despite the rain.

"Yes, our fearless Kommandant, Alois Bielas," Henri Akoka laughed, "the rotund veteran of the Great War, a survivor of the Battle at Verdun in 1916, has been saddled with the care of prisoners. He'll never receive the Iron Cross or be invited to a state dinner with *der Führer* because he is too nice, not mean enough. No, he runs a fine prison camp. And the ever faithful Hauptmann, Karl Albert Brüll, the German guard with a heart. It couldn't be lovelier. Why would I ever want to escape?"

"Oh, it's just lovely here," Corporal Pasquier nodded, opening his hands indicating the dreary weather. "Lovelier than a day in Paris."

"*Mai Oui*," Lieutenant Simon Busseron puffed on his pipe, biting the stem, "We French should be back in gay Paris, sipping coffee on La Rive Gauche of the Seine, preparing to take in an opera by week's end."

*****

October 1940

The days grew shorter, the shadows lengthened, and the weather turned colder as low clouds wept an ugly sleet.

With each passing day rain, sleet, and brisk winds had striped autumn of its former glory as each tree in turn gave up its ghost. The dying leaves had turned from their colorful splendor and fallen to earth, winter's revenge upon the beauty of spring and the life of summer. Birds feverishly flitted about foraging for food amid the falling and blowing whirlwind of dead leaves.

Even the oak trees, which were the last to let go of their leaves, holding out hope against the death of winter, had already dropped their foliage, a harbinger of worse weather and darker days to come.

Messiaen continued to receive fewer and fewer letters from his wife Claire. She was serving as both mother and father to a very active toddler. She included a photograph of her and Pascal. The premature wrinkles under her eyes and far off look worried Messiaen. Meanwhile, Pascal, with his curly blonde hair, revealed a budding personality. Oh, how Messiaen longed to fly like a bird to the mountains and be with his wife and son.

Thanks to Hauptmann Brüll, Messiaen was able to take refuge in the priests' barracks to have time for prayer and composing. On Sundays, Messiaen was practically absent from the camp: he spent his day praying in the chapel barracks.

Red Cross rations of potatoes, cabbage and turnips began to arrive, but they were still insufficient for so many prisoners. The men often passed the time by recounting their favorite meals to one another day and night.

"Olivier, do you remember having duck *à l'orange?*" Pasquier asked Messiaen in the mess hall. He went on detailing the recipe for the dish.

"*Si vous plaît*, you are a cruel man," Messiaen said, sipping his ersatz coffee. "There is no chicken in this chicken soup and there is no coffee in this coffee."

"I'd rather drink piss than this ersatz shit!" Le Boulaire said, lighting a cigarette.

"All right," Henri Akoka said, "Give me your cup and I'll fill it up."

Le Boulaire tossed the cup to Akoka who started to unzip his pants.

The men laughed, but it was not a hearty laugh, but a laugh to cover their grief and homesickness for as long as they laughed they would not weep.

Unfortunately, Messiaen's health had been compromised along with the other men. Messiaen's hair was falling out, his gums ached and several of his teeth were loose. His hands were swollen and irritated from the cold and damp conditions. His clothes went unlaundered for weeks at a time and lice were as common as bedbugs.

The Red Cross rations of cigarettes were guarded and doled out like gold coins. There were some of the French who could speak German and they would barter with the guards with a wristwatch or other belongings, but cigarettes were the wampum of the Stalag.

Messiaen's thoughts returned to his musical composition. The idea of Christ as the source of Eternity – Eternal Life Himself – returned time and time again. He believed with all his being that though evil may flourish, the mystery of God would be revealed. Wickedness and evil seem to hold sway, but in the end, God would conquer evil.

He shared his thoughts with Etienne Pasquier. "There are moments when I fear I have forgotten everything about music, that I will never again be capable of doing another harmonic analysis, never again be able to compose."

"Don't be ridiculous, Olivier, your solace is in that backpack of yours," Pasquier said, reassuringly.

"Ah, the Holy Scriptures, the Imitation of Christ, and my musical scores," Messiaen smiled. "You are right. Yet even I have my moments of doubt in this most unnatural of places. Then I remember that prayer is the ultimate weapon in the face of such evil. I must trust that it is God's will for me to be where I am.

"Akoka believes it is God's will that he should escape," Pasquier shook his head.

"I will pray he is safely delivered," Messiaen said to Pasquier knowing that Akoka was planning an escape. "I pray for him daily, my Jewish Trotskyite friend. Though how I wish for him to remain. How else will my quartet be a quartet? He is my clarinetist."

*****

While the October rains turned to snow, the French and Germans alike grew accustomed to Le Boulaire's violin and Akoka's clarinet, so they took up a collection from both prisoners and the German guards to purchase a used cello for Pasquier. The prisoners had donated 65 marks from their earnings alone and, much to Pasquier's amazement, Kommandant Bielas gave Hauptmann Brüll permission to drive Pasquier into the town of Görlitz to purchase the cello.

The streets of Görlitz were narrow; the cars shared the road with horses and horse-drawn carts, and bicyclists. The effects of the war were clear. Pasquier took note of the storefronts that were either broken down, boarded-up, or burnt. "Those were the Jewish businesses owned by Jews," Brüll said looking away. "The Jews are being relocated."

That's all that was said.

Brüll drove him to a music store where used musical instruments were for sale. The owner actually made musical instruments as well. Not only that, but Brüll purchased Pasquier a cello, bow, rosin and an extra set of strings and a new set of strings for Le Boulaire's violin. He also picked up several pads of music sheets, pencils, and erasers for Messiaen.

"I could kiss you, Brüll," Pasquier said to Brüll, referring to the cello purchase as they rode back to Stalag 8A.

"You crazy Frenchman," Brüll laughed. "Just play Bach's Cello Suites for me and that will suffice."

"I understand," Pasquier nodded and smiled as he thought of the works for cello by Johann Sebastian Bach. "It's been too long since I played Bach."

Upon Brüll and Pasquier's return to Stalag 8A, the prisoners begged Pasquier to play the cello for hours. He played Saint-Saens Swan from the carnival of the animals, Bach's Suites for Solo Cello, Schubert's Ave Maria, and some other popular pieces.

Some of the men cried for joy.

*****

1 November 1940

A heavy snow on the eve of All Saints brightened the camp. Lieutenant Simon Busseron had also secured a copy of Winston Churchill's speech from 21 October. Busseron read it aloud to the men before lights out.

"Never will I believe that the soul of France is dead! Never will I believe that her place amongst the greatest nations of the world has been lost forever.

"Remember that we shall never stop, never weary, and never give in . . . We seek to beat the life and soul out of Hitler and Hitlerism. That alone - that all the time - that to the end. Those French who are in the French Empire, and those who are in the so-called unoccupied France, may see their way from time to time to useful action. I will not go into details...hostile ears are listening...

"Good night then: Sleep to gather strength for the morning. For the morning will come. Brightly it will shine on the brave and true, kindly upon all who suffer for the cause, glorious upon the tombs of heroes. Thus will shine the dawn.

"Vive La France!"

With the words of Churchill fresh in their minds and the warmth of the music in their hearts, many of the men went to bed hopeful for the first time since their imprisonment despite the onslaught of an early cold and bitter winter.

For Messiaen there were moments of grace, sun on the blanket of snow, the songs and calls of birds, yet there were also those moments where he seemed without hope and denied his feelings.

Messiaen, reflecting in the dark at night, had vivid memories and the constant thought of his wife and son. In his mind he went to Mass and played the organ; he bounced Pascal on his knee and enjoyed evenings with his wife as she composed and played the violin while he accompanied her on the piano; and he conducted symphonies and attended concerts, yet wept as the dreams that seemed so real gave way to the harsh reality of barbed wire, and nightmarish images of his wife being ravaged by Nazis and both her and his son being shot and killed.

*****

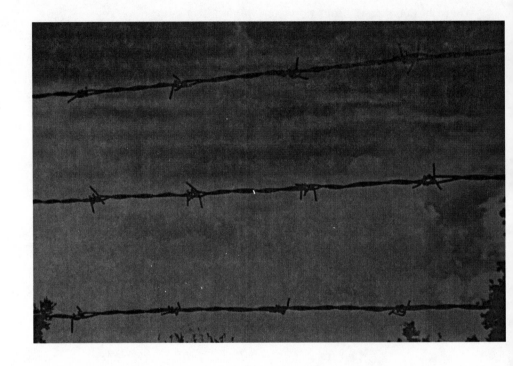

"I write music for the same reason
apple trees bear apples–
It is simply what I do.
Music gives me a means
of expressing my deep feelings
about nature, love, and God."
- Olivier Messiaen

Chapter 13

Providence

November 1940

Despite the early snow, by the end of the year more than 50 barracks huts had been built, including two large kitchens. A dozen or more of the barracks were reserved for the guards and the Command Post. With the construction of the new barracks, the Polish and Czechoslovakian prisoners dwelling in tents were quite relieved.

Messiaen and the other men continued to lose their hair and teeth owing to the primitive conditions and poor diet of only one meal per day – stale bread made mostly of sawdust and a soup with few ingredients save the watered-down broth. Particularly painful were chilblains of the hands and feet caused by the extreme damp cold, freezing temperatures, and snow.

Some of the soldiers kept themselves busy "reading," while others were "down" with something. These were their code words for the men on the Escape Committee who were digging tunnels to get the hell out of the Stalag. Pails, tin cups, wooden spoons, bowls, and anything else that could be used for digging, continued to go missing from the kitchen. The German ferrets, the guards who crawled under the barracks looking for tunnels or signs of digging, increased their vigil.

It was not uncommon for the Germans to conduct an occasional search or inspection of barracks during an impromptu roll call. At first such inspections were perfunctory, but by November, following several escapes, they became regular and each prisoner had to be accounted for twice daily.

*****

While the other three musicians now had their instruments, Messiaen was still without his piano. Messiaen led his three musicians to the latrine where they now regularly practiced.

"I have written a little trio for the three of you," Messiaen announced to his musicians the moisture of his breath lingering in the cold air before disappearing. "It is rather unpretentious."

"Easy for you to say," Akoka replied, glancing at the clarinetist section. "It's as unpretentious as you and your *Abime des Oiseaux*."

"It is part of a larger quartet I am working on," Messiaen said as he paged through his manuscript.

"A quartet?" asked Le Boulaire as he breathed through his thumbs into his interlocked fingers.

"Yes, a quartet for piano, cello, clarinet and violin."

"Aren't you missing a piano?" Le Boulaire asked, reaching for his cigarette stash.

"A trivial matter," Messiaen smiled, pushing his glasses back up his nose.

"How in hell can you have a quartet without a piano?" Le Boulaire asked, lighting a cigarette.

"Don't worry. God will provide. I am still alive, *non*? Besides, I have it all here in my head." Messiaen tapped his right forefinger against his forehead. "It will work. Trust the music."

"What musical language is this?" Pasquier said, perusing the bars and notes.

"Mine," Messiaen replied, smiling.

"It is ametrical?" Pasquier said more as a question.

"*Oui*." Messiaen nodded enthusiastically, fingering the buttons of his jacket as he explained, "It is about the ending of concepts of past and future: the end of time and the beginning of eternity."

"*Mais oui*, of course," laughed Akoka, as he examined his clarinet. "Music is sound and silence."

"*Oui*. Solemn silence, the mysterious reality of eternity–God's Time."

"Incomprehensible," Akoka shook his head as he took out his pack of cigarettes, placed one in his mouth, and offered Pasquier one as well.

"Precisely my point," Messiaen answered. "I was inspired by the angel of the apocalypse."

"From the Book of the Apocalypse?" asked Pasquier, getting a light from Akoka.

"*Oui.*"

"Cataclysm and catastrophe; the beast and the anti-Christ?" Pasquier continued, his lit cigarette balancing between his lips.

"*Non, non*, the book of the Apocalypse is much more than that," Messiaen asserted. "Much more. Full of light and silence. When we pray the *Glória Patria*, we say *Glória Patri, et Fílio, et Spirítui Sancto. Sicut erat in princípio, et nunc et semper et in saecula saeculórum.* But isn't there something not quite right, theologically, about that statement? To speak of God, the Eternal Being as 'was' and 'will be' seems improper for God since those two words imply becoming in time. There is no beginning in God. God is, and in truth, we should say is always and forever. Eternity does not begin. It always is. Time, however, had a beginning and it will be brought to an end—at the apocalypse."

"I thought you taught music," Akoka said, his cigarette between his fingers, "not philosophy and theology."

"Oh, but it is all connected, no?" He removed his glasses. "Don't you see?"

"Not really," Akoka rolled his eyes, taking a hit from his smoke. "I think the lack of food has made you delirious."

"I have food of which you do not know," Messiaen replaced his glasses.

"You have food?" Henri Akoka asked, removing his cigarette from his mouth.

"No," Messiaen sighed. "It is a reference to the gospel of St. John."

"Figures," Akoka replied. "Look, at the rate you are going, you're going to put the chaplain out of a job and they'll send him to one of the work camps."

"*Oui.* One chaplain is enough," Le Boulaire laughed, taking his violin from its case.

"But there is something brilliant in his music," Pasquier added, as he removed his cello from its case and rosined the bow. "Even if Olivier denies the double entendre about the end of time and merely wishes to eliminate classical musical time, we can delight in the image of judgment day in our own time when we shall be delivered and the Nazis routed."

"Or ultimately on the last day when the perpetrators of evil will have to render an account of their deeds to the Almighty," Messiaen said, looking up from his musical score, his eyes unblinking, and voice certain.

"All right, enough theology," Le Boulaire said, placing his bow on the strings of his violin. "Let's play."

"*Merci*," Messiaen nodded as he made sure each man was on the same page.

*****

Messiaen met with Abbé Jean Brossard, the French priest and military chaplain taken prisoner near Verdun. Abbé Brossard was a priest nearly six feet tall, his eyes hazel, his black hair parted on his left and combed over, revealing his forehead. His face was ruddy, with a perpetual five o'clock shadow. He was a virile priest, one who was familiar with hard work and, now, deprivation and suffering. He always wore his black soutane, its fascia about his stomach and its fringed ends dangling down along his left side.

Under a milky sky that matched the snow on the ground, the two men walked and talked one afternoon.

"I am taken by all things musical," Messiaen said as they walked together. "Even my prayer is musical. It is in the present moment where all time is still. The past is past; the future has yet to be: all is now."

"Ah, *oui*, kairos time and chronos time," Brossard reflected, smoking his cigarette.

"Eternity is not a long period of time; it is no time at all," Messiaen answered. "The ever present moment."

"*Oui*. I understand. Time here at Stalag 8A moves incredibly slowly," Brossard proffered.

"I feel as if I am living a monastic existence of sorts." Messiaen rubbed his forehead with the fingers of his right hand. "Where time is marked by chant in the church, for me the serenely soaring strain of the

116

violin and cello teaches us that there is a way to live that transcends this world of chaos and war."

Abbé Brossard glanced at him. "Why do you do what you do? Why do you compose?"

"I am a composer because I love music." Messiaen's face was illumined as his voice became firm and distinct. "I write music for the same reason apple trees bear apples: it is simply what I do. Music gives me a means of expressing my deep feelings about nature, love, and God. My calling to be an artist and a Christian are one and the same vocation."

Messiaen turned to Abbé Brossard, placing his left hand on the priest's right shoulder. "I am a Christian because I love God – and believe. Like Saint Peter walking on water, we must not doubt and begin to drown. As for the miracle of Pasquier, Akoka, and Le Boulaire being in this camp at precisely the right place and right time – and even the good fortune of being granted permission to have instruments – I don't believe in chance. I believe in Providence. God leaves nothing to chance." Messiaen faced Brossard.

"Is it not our hope – our calling to be caught up to God in Christ, where Christ is all and is in all?" Abbé Brossard pondered, stopping momentarily. "We are God's children now. What we shall later be has not yet come to light. We know that when it does come to light we shall be like him, for we shall see him as he is. As the psalmist wrote: 'O Lord, in your light we see light itself.'"

"Through my music I pray to sing the gift of the divine essence," Messiaen added, placing his hands over his heart. "What I believe in, what I hope for, what I love – is God. My musical ability is a great gift, but my faith is the foremost gift. Of this I am sure. One of my professors told me something very important early in my academic career, at a time when I regarded my musical gifts with too much vainglory. I had been in the small town of Nantes where all regarded me as a prodigy – a second Mozart – but once in Paris, Professor Gallon told me, 'You are nothing here. You know nothing. Learn your place'. He was correct. Ever since then I have learned my place." Messiaen stroked his neck and chin, deep in thought.

"That was one of the most valuable lessons in humility that I ever learned. I learned that I was a young idiot. Perhaps it is the only lesson I won't regret at the hour of my death. Yet I doubt my gift at times. I feel as if my music isn't understood or appreciated. And I fear that all I am doing is in vain."

"All work done for the Lord is never in vain," Abbé Brossard said. "Fear not. Yet beware of the sin of pride. Remain humble and all shall be well."

Messiaen then explained the situation with his wife and his concern for her health.

"Love is real. Do not deny it. Yet love entails death to self. Christ died that we might live. And if we embrace Christ we must also embrace his pain and death. Intimacy can lead to loss and even abandonment. And loss is very real. We must not deny loss. Entrust Claire to the care of Divine Providence," Brossard said. "It is all you can do."

The two returned to the chapel barracks.

*****

Chapter 14

The Piano

After evening roll call, Messiaen, Pasquier, and Akoka walked the snowy grounds. In the midst of the bleak surroundings the sky had cleared and they beheld a group of chirping sparrows darting and diving in the vesper sun.

"Why does the bird sing?" Messiaen asked. "Is he not free? His nature is to give glory to his maker. Did not Christ say, 'Look at the birds of the air. They neither sow nor reap, they gather nothing into barns, yet the heavenly Father feeds them. Worry not about tomorrow. Tomorrow will take care of itself. Today has enough troubles of its own'?"

Messiaen's rosary dangled from his right hand. "Tomorrow does not even exist. All we have is the eternal moment of now. His kingdom has come. Nature manifests aspects of God's divinity and draws us to Him. Take the beauty of birdsong, the color and fragrance of flowers and wildflowers, and light itself. All manifest the manifold graces of God. Even the glistening snow has a music all its own."

"I wish I had your faith," Pasquier said as he turned and worked to light his cigarette against the cold wind.

"It isn't mine; it is a gift," Messiaen replied, pressing the beads of the rosary between his thumb and index finger. "And I share it with you for God shares it with me." He closed his eyes and breathed in deeply.

"Oh, Etienne," Messiaen opened his eyes and gazed intently at Pasquier. "Dare to peer into eternity. For the Lord has mercy. He brings back Israel's exiles; he binds up all their wounds. He brings up from the depths of the nether world and the great abyss. In Him do our hearts find joy."

"You are bold!" Henri Akoka said. "The psalms are at the heart of every Jew's prayer."

"And for Catholics as well. Yet it is not I who am bold. It isn't even in my temperament to be audacious by any means. Rather it is the Holy

Spirit of God that gives me such confidence and the fortitude to speak thus." Suddenly, Messiaen felt a warmth fill his heart that seemed to thaw the grimy cold.

"Henri, you have the gift of music," Messiaen continued. "Do you not?"

"My father is a musician," Henri Akoka answered, revealing a cigarette from his shirt pocket. "He plays the trumpet, violin, and piano. He joined the circus as a teenager when the circus came through his village in Algeria. He went on tour in Italy and southern France playing the trumpet." Akoka shielded his cigarette from the wind and lit it. "Later he decided to move his family to France so all of us children could become professional musicians. He always said, 'In life, one must make music. One cannot go through life without making music.' It is a beautiful thought, no?" He puffed on his cigarette and looked at Messiaen.

"I should like to meet your father when all this dirty business of war is over," Messiaen smiled as they neared the snowy drifts near the fence.

"How can you go on believing, Olivier?" Henri Akoka asked, exhaling smoke which lingered in the frigid air. "Look at all the suffering! God does not see our plight or hear our cries!"

"Ah, but he does; He came in order to suffer with us. Oftentimes when we think God is far off, it is then that He is nearest to us. Indeed, his body is even now racked with pain, impaled upon the gibbet of the cross."

"I'll never understand you, my friend, but I love you," Akoka inhaled another draft from his smoke.

"And I love you, my Jewish Trotskyite brother."

The men continued to walk along, each lost in thought.

"Many Catholics have gone along with Hitler and hate Jews," Pasquier said to Messiaen, "Why not you?"

"Not all Catholics have betrayed their faith for the Nazi Party," Messiaen replied. "Christ our Savior was a Jew. If I hate you, then I hate him. We are to love all men as brothers, even the barbaric Nazis. Even the Nazis."

"Well, you're on your own there, Olivier," snorted Akoka. "They hate us Jews. Mark my word, they intend to destroy us. Don't ask me how, but I have heard stories and I am convinced that these concentration camps, or as the Nazis prefer – 'relocation centers' – are not merely to keep us quarantined."

"Pray, my friend," Messiaen said as he beheld the crisp blue evening sky. "Pray."

"You can pray for me. I intend to escape. I'm digging my way out of this hell-hole if it's the last thing I do. Pray that I escape."

"And what if they find you?"

"I'll play my clarinet for them and charm them into returning me to Paris or Marseilles."

"You cannot be serious about tunneling out?" Messiaen asked as he squinted in the setting sun, its pinks and oranges glistening on the snow.

"I've never been more serious in my life," Akoka replied, his jaw firmly set. "I cannot recall life without this damned barbed wire. Now, Oli, you'd better hurry up with your composition because I'm busting out of this bird cage. You can come with me. Let's get out of here and get back to Paris where we belong."

"Henri, we are 1400 kilometers from Paris," Messiaen said before pausing.

"But Switzerland is a mere 900 kilometers," Akoka smiled. He took the cigarette from his mouth, resting it between his right index and middle fingers, and exhaled upward.

"*Merely* 900?" Messiaen looked aghast.

"*Oui*," Akoka replied, still smiling as if he already had his escape planned.

"Can't you wait until after the première?" Messiaen tilted his head and laughed. "Besides, it's winter."

"The snow doesn't stop the birds, does it?" Akoka challenged him. "Now is our time to fly."

"Like a bird," Messiaen said quietly.

"*Oui*. So finish the quartet."

"I cannot rush genius."

"Then allow me," Akoka said with a laugh, restoring his cigarette to his mouth.

"It is a quartet."

"Then finish it or it will have to be a trio."

"A trio? I need your clarinet," Messiaen said as he patted Akoka on the shoulder.

"And the Nazis are imprisoning my people. I must escape in order to sabotage Hitler's plans."

"I have faith in God," Messiaen said.

"I have faith in Man," Akoka replied, taking a deep smoke.

"Which men?" asked Messiaen.

"Well, certainly not the Nazis, but you know what I mean."

"I have accepted my situation," Messiaen said. "In it I must find the will of God."

"Well, while you're working on finding God's will, I'm going to be finding a way out of this place," Akoka chuckled. "A prisoner is intended for escape."

"I will continue to pray for you," Messiaen assured him, holding his breath.

"I'd much rather that you'd help me tunnel out," Akoka said as he scooted his feet through a drift of virgin snow.

"But you're a Jew," Messiaen cautioned.

"All the more reason for me to escape from the Germans."

"Into the hands of the Gestapo or SS?" Messiaen replied with another question.

"Look around, Oli," Akoka gesticulated passionately. "This isn't exactly Paris!"

Messiaen and Pasquier laughed.

"Though you are Jewish," Pasquier said, "the German guards handle you with care, probably to let the Red Cross believe that the Nazis care for all allied prisoners of war equally – Gentiles and Jews."

"As long as you have the French uniform, or at least are a prisoner of war, you are safe," Messiaen explained. "However, if you escape, they will likely send you to Dachau, Buchenwald, Auschwitz, or one of the camps. Trust me, the SS is no friend to the Jews or anyone opposed to *der Führer.* Jewish civilians are at risk of deportation. You may be safer here than back in France."

"Oli is right," Pasquier said.

"Safe?" Akoka snapped, removing his cigarette again. "The SS wants all Jews to be deported to the camps. There are many rumors circulating." Akoka shook his head and continued, "So while the SS determines my fate, I plan on escaping from this hell-hole and returning to occupied France without fear. I have family that needs me and a country that must be freed from tyranny. I have nothing left to fear." He took one last long drag from the cigarette and flicked it away, watching it fall to the ground where it smoldered in the slush.

*****

As part of maintaining one's sanity, various academic classes were offered to the prisoners. Messiaen as a professor was asked to teach a music class. Gratefully, he took the opportunity to explain Gregorian chant to some of the prisoners in the theatre barracks.

"Melismas. *Oui,* the incredible melisma. It is the gentle rise and fall of the voiced word; such melody, the cadence, based on the words of the scripture, for the text guides the melody. There is no time, rather the words receive however many notes they need. Out of silence comes the single voice of many singers, no one voice dominates the other, every note is as important as the other, the message of the text is conveyed by the musical line. The mystery of the Latin, even when fully understood, nurtures our souls in a sacramental way when it is sung. The equal duration and equal volume for each note of the chant is timeless as well."

The men asked no questions as they pondered Messiaen's words.

"Just as divine reading, *lectio divina,* forms the hearer, the chanted word forms the faith of the hearer. The music is set to the Word. There is a mystery in the Word that is never quite exhausted; its meaning and presence never fully understood or extracted, as is the eternal spring, Christ Himself, who is the Word made flesh. When one chants the scripture, God sings through him or her, rather than merely singing *to* God or only singing *about* God.

"The purpose of music is to open the human person to the reality of the natural order through the use of reason. St. William of Auvergne wrote, 'When you consider the order and magnificence of the Universe, you will find it to be like a great beautiful canticle and the wondrous variety of its creatures to be a symphony of joy and harmony.'"

Messiaen was chanting one of the psalms when suddenly Etienne Pasquier entered the room. "Olivier! Olivier! I think you need to come see something."

"What is it?" Messiaen was genuinely perturbed, being interrupted in the middle of a psalm.

"Just come with me," Pasquier motioned eagerly. "Trust me. You'll want to see this."

"Please excuse me, gentlemen," Messiaen said to the few men seated at the tables in front of him. "Class dismissed. We will meet again tomorrow."

Pasquier led Messiaen across the slushy yard and to the front gate of the Stalag where a German military transport truck idled in front of the Kommandant's quarters.

"This better be important," Messiaen said, his feet getting wet and cold as he sloshed through the slushy snow.

"It is," Pasquier said with a peculiar glee. "Trust me, it is."

As they approached the truck, Pasquier took him around the back of it. Messiaen could hardly believe his eyes. Hauptmann Brüll and Lieutenant Schmitt and two other German soldiers were wrestling an old upright piano out of the truck.

"Damn! I can't believe we're going to all this trouble for one prisoner!" Schmitt said angrily before seeing Messiaen and Pasquier come around the back of the truck.

"I hope you play this son-of-a-bitch," Schmitt said to Messiaen, as he sweated and grunted maneuvering the piano to a wheeled cart in the miry mud-stained slush.

Messiaen's jaw felt numb and his tongue useless, incredulous at the sight of a piano. "I shall...I shall," he stuttered, "try to play it to my best ability."

"That is what we want to hear," Kommandant Bielas proclaimed as he stepped out onto the front steps of his quarters and clasped Messiaen on the right shoulder. "The Wehrmacht has once more provided for the needs of its prisoners."

"*Ja wohl*," Messiaen said, examining the instrument. "And I will not disappoint – just don't drop it, Lieutenant Schmitt."

"I am hoping that you and your musicians can provide us all with musical entertainment," Bielas continued, tugging on his left earlobe. "The war continues to drag on and it appears we will be spending our winter months here. Therefore, it is our wish that our situation here be made as bearable as possible. With that in mind I have instructed that the recreation barracks be used as the theatre and you and your men will perform a concert every Saturday night at 1800 hours. Hauptmann Brüll will see to it that all is in order and your needs are provided for."

"*Danke schön! Merci beaucoup!*" Messiaen replied, tipping his cap to the Kommandant.

"You don't have to be that excited," Pasquier whispered. "He is a German, you know. The Nazis aren't exactly the wise men bearing gifts."

The piano was taken to Barracks 27. It had a couple of broken strings, several keys that stuck, and it was a bit out of tune, but it was still welcomed with joy. Brüll even gave Messiaen some musical scores of Beethoven, Mozart, and Chopin.

One of the first pieces Messiaen, Boulaire and Pasquier performed for the prisoners was a quartet version of Beethoven's Seventh Symphony. Even some of the German guards attended the show that first Saturday night of November.

The music of the solo violin, cello, clarinet, or piano and sonatas, trios, and quartet works was a welcome respite from the starkness of exile in a Stalag.

Messiaen and the others played Mozart, Ravel, Bach, Beethoven, Brahms, Chopin, and Debussy. Messiaen even played some variations on themes of Prokofiev, and Pasquier obtained a copy of the Cello Sonata by Sergei Rachmaninoff.

Messiaen performed his Preludes, which he had first published in 1928 and 1929. He gave the men enough of the classics, but wanted to stretch their musical horizons by incorporating French Impressionism and avant-garde modern works, ever seeking for his own music to be appreciated.

Some argued that the motive behind the Germans allowing for such concerts was in order to maintain a good image in the French press.

"They want the world to see how cultural the Nazis can be. 'Why, France is the same as before,'" Le Boulaire sneered during rehearsal before one of the shows. "We're playing right into their hands. We're the dupes."

"If more men would take up a violin or clarinet rather than a rifle or grenade," Messiaen philosophized, as he fingered the white and black keys of the piano, "the world would be a far, far better place."

*****

Chapter 15

Escapee

One November evening, Henri Akoka failed to show for rehearsal. Instead, Lieutenant Simon Busseron and Sergeant Jacques Chevalier appeared in the theatre barracks instead.

"Where's Henri Akoka?" Messiaen asked as he was preparing for a version of Mozart's Clarinet Concerto for solo piano and clarinet.

"He won't be practicing with you," Busseron removed his cap and pursed his lips around the stem of his Meerschaum pipe.

"Why not?"

"He's *down*." Busseron popped his lips three times, releasing three perfect smoke rings from the bowl of his pipe.

"*Down*? Is he ill?" Messiaen asked, laying aside his music sheets.

"Not quite," Sergeant Jacques Chevalier answered, removed his cap, revealing his tousled brown hair.

"Akoka has disappeared," Busseron answered, removing his pipe from his mouth. "Rumor has it that he has become a gopher."

"A gopher?" Messiaen asked, unsure what it meant.

"He tunneled out," Chevalier made it clear.

"*Non, non!*" Messiaen shook his head, visibly agitated. "I need him for the quartet."

"I think you just became a trio," Chevalier laughed, as he put his cap back on.

"Lucky bastard," Le Boulaire replied, lowering his violin from his chin.

"If it is any consolation," Busseron said, "Kommandant Bielas told the soldiers, 'Find the Jewish clarinetist, but bring him back alive.'"

"Is your Jewish friend not aware that he'll likely be safer here with us than in France under the Vichy rule?" Chevalier asked.

"*Mon Dieu*. Pray for Henri." Messiaen turned to Pasquier and Le Boulaire. "Etienne, we will have to play that cello sonata we practiced last evening. Jean, you can play some of your favorite violin solo works. Then the three of us will play a trio."

*****

Recent news of the war obtained through the clandestine use of the wireless reported that the war wasn't going well for Britain. The U.S. still remained out of the war even though London was burning nightly and the Luftwaffe was claiming victory. Beginning in October, the Vichy government had enacted anti-Semitic laws. And with each escape from one of the Stalags, the Gestapo and SS were making more periodic visits to the camps.

The Red Cross packages were few and far between and the men complained at mail call.

"Again," the German Lieutenant Schmitt shouted in rage, "The Red Cross didn't plan on feeding and supplying the entire f—ing French army!

"But the Geneva Convention requires prisoners of war to be supplied with clothes, food, footwear, underwear and blankets!" Busseron argued, clenching his pipe between his teeth.

"Is that right?" Schmitt asked, pointing his rifle at Busseron. "Well, if you haven't noticed there's a war on! So hopefully Saint Nicholas will bring you what you want because neither the German army nor the Red Cross has anything to spare this year."

"I'd write Saint Nicholas a letter, you dumbass German," Chevalier countered, "but since the mail isn't moving I'd doubt he'd get it in time for Christmas."

"At least we agree on something," Schmitt laughed, shoving his machine gun into Chevalier's back. "Except you are the *Dumpfbacke*. I'm not the one who's in prison." Schmitt spat on the barrack's floor at Chevalier's feet before kicking the door open to leave.

Though the Germans treated the French with some respect, each prisoner lived in constant fear of being killed or shot on sight by a Nazi guard. There was a terrible desensitization to evil and violence toward the human person. Human life meant nothing to these men. It was a world where the value of human life and human dignity no longer mattered and was no longer being recognized.

The apathy among the men grew worse with the lack of cigarettes and real coffee; sleep deprivation and hunger; and the rats and lice. Regardless of whether the men were respectable businessmen, musicians, professors, or bricklayers, plumbers, or carpenters, they had all been reduced to nothing.

However, Messiaen held on to his conviction that the Nazis could imprison a man, but could not remove his freedom to embrace faith, hope, and charity – even in the face of great adversity or horrendous evil.

*****

11 November 1940

After midnight on the anniversary of Armistice Day marking the end of the Great War, the brutal reality of life in the Stalag returned. It was Sergeant Schmitt pounding on the door of Barracks 19A.

"Out, Out! *Raus! Raus! Macht schnell!*" Schmitt's voice pierced the darkness. "The Gestapo is here!"

"Great, now the Gestapo's inquisition begins!" Le Boulaire said, as he roused from slumber.

"No more privileges!" Schmitt declared, still pounding.

"We know you're only saying that because you have to," Chevalier said.

"Shut it," Schmitt pointed the machine gun at him. "Out! Out!"

The men stepped outside only to be pelted with freezing rain as they tramped out into the icy mud and filthy snow.

Le Boulaire looked around and noticed that Messiaen was not in the line.

"Where is the composer?" Brüll leaned in and asked him.

"I think he may be back at Barracks 27."

"It's Saturday night, Lieutenant Schmitt," Chevalier laughed, "Where's your sense of humor? And it's sleeting? Can't this wait till morning?"

Unexpectedly, an SS officer in a black leather trench coat appeared around the corner of Barracks 19A.

The men's posture immediately straightened and they stopped their mouths as they realized this was not one of Schmitt's ruses. They meekly obeyed.

"Missing pails, cups, and serving spoons, now even some shovels are missing!" the highly decorated SS officer angrily shouted. His swastika armband stood out in the light of the camp searchlights. The Nazi symbol had never been more visible or numerous – nor more formidable. "What kind of a prison is the Wehrmacht's Heer running here?! Are the inmates in charge of the prison?! Now we hear of escapes gone unchecked!" He spat his words out, his odious breath angrily hanging in the icy mist.

Kommandant Bielas said nothing as his tight-lipped face was buffeted by the blowing sleet. The rumors that both Bielas and Brüll were on report due to Akoka's escape seemed to have been beautifully confirmed by the Gestapo's midnight visit.

As the men lined up for roll call, the Gestapo began counting the men. Within minutes the SS officers begin shouting Messiaen's number. "Prisoner 35333! Number 35333!"

There was no answer.

"Who knows the whereabouts of this prisoner?!" the chief SS officer's words were again as visible as they were audible.

"*Mon Dieu!*" Lieutenant Busseron sighed loudly. "Where the hell is the old man? The SS doesn't deal well with tardiness."

"I want information! Who is this prisoner number 35333?" the SS officer shouted at Brüll who was conversing with Kommandant Bielas.

Sergeant Schmitt cried aloud: "Olivier Messiaen!"

The men were made to stand in the wind, sleet and snow as the ferrets crawled under every barracks and the SS rifled through the prisoners belongings.

The men watched Hauptmann Brüll quickly make his way toward Barracks 27.

A few minutes later Brüll appeared, hurriedly pushing Olivier Messiaen forward with a rifle to his back; in turn several SS officers followed Brüll.

"Even Brüll's acting like a Nazi tonight!" Pasquier said under his breath.

"I wonder what the hell Messiaen is thinking?" Chevalier asked. "What was he doing back there at this hour?"

"Who knows?" Pasquier asked. "He was probably praying or composing – or both."

"He gets so lost in his thoughts he likely never heard the wake-up call or else he was asleep," Le Boulaire said.

"Well, either way, he's awake now. Look!" said Chevalier, pointing to Messiaen being marched forward through the snowy slush.

Messiaen's uncombed hair blew in the cold, icy wind as he struggled to keep warm and took up his usual place in the middle of the camp.

"There was found a hidden radio in one of the barracks tonight!" The SS officer shouted loudly to the assembled prisoners. "And several men from this camp escaped earlier this week, but we found them – or they found us. Some will be returning. Others will not. They are no more."

Messiaen, Pasquier, Le Boulaire, Busseron, and Chevalier all turned and looked at one another. None of them said anything, but the name Henri Akoka was on all of their lips.

"We will no longer tolerate such blatant disregard for the rule of law," the SS officer continued his rant. "The German is the strongest race of men: not the French, not the Pole."

On the other side of the fence, the men could see some German soldiers viciously abusing and beating the Polish and Czechoslovakian prisoners of war.

"You French have received kind treatment from your German conquerors. Is escape any way to repay our kindness?"

No one answered, but Chevalier could be heard murmuring under his breath, "Spare us the drama, you Nazi pigs! Bastard Germans!"

"Now you men will stand here in the cold, sleet, and snow for as long as it takes my men to find any other contraband! So enjoy the German weather, my French citizens of the Third Reich. This will teach you and your Resistance to learn your place in this world. The Third Reich will last a thousand years!"

Suddenly machine gun rang out. Several Polish and Czech prisoners dropped to the ground on the other side of the fence.

"Don't make us use these methods among the cooperative French!" The Gestapo chief yelled.

Some of the French soldiers laughed when the shots rang out. In the insanity of war, humor was often a means for a man to get through the brutality and violence.

"Poor bastards," Busseron said loud enough for most of the prisoners to hear but not loud enough for the Gestapo to care.

Under the bright searchlights, the grey snow turned a crimson red framing the bodies of the dead men.

Messiaen prayed for Henri Akoka. He prayed first and foremost that he wasn't dead. But if he was dead, then he prayed for the repose of his soul and for the family he had left behind.

*****

Due to the continued lack of proper nutrition, Messiaen began to have bizarre dreams. Images of the angel of the Apocalypse with a rainbow encircling his head and the purple and greens of the aurora borealis kept recurring in his mind. There was a sense of desolation and fear. Would he live to see his wife again? Would he live to see his son Pascal? There were some in the camp who questioned whether this was the end of time and the final battle with the anti-Christ.

Survival was the one thing on their minds. Many of the men lay in their bunks, glassy-eyed and sullen as they smoked their way through the days. Some were surviving only on cigarettes. The cigarette smoke was thick. It reminded Messiaen of the sweet cloud of incense at Benediction and vespers at *Sainte Trinité* Church save that of the smell. Some showered when the water was hot in an attempt to soothe their souls.

Messiaen reflected upon his own suffering and wrote in his journal.

The Lord God has seen fit to choose me for some specific purpose—even here amid the desolation of war and the darkness of this camp. He has allowed me to share in His sufferings. I believe that in all of these events there is a higher purpose. I must believe this. Obedience under difficult and unjust conditions embraces suffering as a pathway to peace and endures it without seeking escape. Those who patiently endure unjust treatment and take up the cross persevere to the end.

Christ's command in Matthew's gospel was his guiding light as he prayerfully pondered the sacred text:

> *But I say to you, offer no resistance to one who is evil. When someone strikes you on your right cheek, turn the other one to him as well. Should anyone press you into service for one mile, go with him for two miles. Love your enemies, and pray for those who persecute you, that you may be children of your heavenly Father, for he makes his sun rise on the bad and the good, and causes rain to fall on the just and the unjust. For if you love those who love you, what recompense will you have? Do not the tax collectors do the same? And if you greet your brothers only, what is unusual about that? Do not the pagans do the same? So be perfect, just as your heavenly Father is perfect* (Matt. 5:39-48).

Messiaen flipped the pages of the Bible to one of the epistles of the Apostle Paul:

> *My grace is sufficient for thee.*

The Epistle of Peter reiterated the theme:

> *If I bear the pain of unjust suffering with consciousness of God, then it is a grace* (1 Peter 4.7-9).

> *For whenever anyone bears the pain of unjust suffering because of consciousness of God, that is a grace. But what credit is there if you are patient when beaten for doing wrong? But if you are*

patient when you suffer for doing what is good, this is a grace before God. For to this you have been called, because Christ also suffered for you, leaving you an example that you should follow in his footsteps. He committed no sin, and no deceit was found in his mouth. When he was insulted, he returned no insult; when he suffered, he did not threaten; instead, he handed himself over to the one who judges justly. He himself bore our sins in his body upon the cross, so that, free from sin, we might live for righteousness. By his wounds you have been healed. For you had gone astray like sheep, but you have now returned to the shepherd and guardian of your souls (1 Peter 2:19-25).

Messiaen continued his own notes:

The body, the senses, are not in opposition to the soul, the spirit. We are bodied spirits. Christ became man, human, that we might share in his divinity, and in the very life of the Holy Trinity! So what of the suffering we experience here? Christ came to suffer with us! Just as there is a suffering even in our joy, so there is joy in our sufferings.

The thought and memory of his Jewish friend, Henri Akoka, remained with Messiaen. He truly loved the man: his sense of humor, his righteous indignation at Nazi oppression, and his love for music. If he had been killed after escaping Stalag 8A, Messiaen would never be able to hear his solo clarinet piece, *Abime des Oiseaux*, the same way since he had written it specifically with Akoka in mind. The clarinet piece he had written for Akoka was already intended as one of the early movements of his quartet for piano, cello, violin, and clarinet.

Pasquier joined Messiaen for dinner that week. Pasquier carefully lit one of his rationed cigarettes and asked Messiaen about the origins for the Quartet he was composing.

"As for the quartet," Messiaen happily answered, "the work was inspired by chapter ten of the book of the Apocalypse. The scroll of the angel was small and as sweet as honey, for it foretold the final victory of good over evil; yet it was sour in the stomach because it announced the sufferings —" Messiaen paused and stared into the distance and laughed to himself, his face bore an mysterious smile and it was hard for Pasquier to tell whether it was a genuine smile or a melancholy expression of resignation. "I have eaten the scroll of the angel," he spoke again, looking at his companion intently. Even Messiaen was uncertain what it all meant, the thoughts of his wife Claire and son Pascal overwhelming him.

"So your music is the result," Pasquier said. "How appropriate for us to play it in the latrines. A lot of your critics would say this is where it belongs."

"That sounds like something Henri would have said," Messiaen said with a chuckle, more to himself than for Pasquier to hear.

"Yes. It is, isn't it," Pasquier coughed as if to clear his throat. "I miss him too."

Messiaen's eyes became teary. "He never ceased to amuse or amaze me."

Chapter 16

Caged Birds

Messiaen was forever with a pen and paper in hand, sketching notes and musical notations.

"Don't you ever think all of your work and writing is a waste of your time?" Le Boulaire asked him as the men prepared to rehearse.

"No. What do I have other than time?" scoffed Messiaen. "Besides, it isn't my time. It never was. Time is a great gift. Music appears useless to many, but it is meaningful. Music gives joy and praise to the Creator. Just as the birds sing their daily songs for all to hear, so I write music for all to hear. The birds rise early each morning and sing for the Lord to their heart's content. The glory of God is a human being fully alive, just as for a bird the glory of God is a bird fully alive and singing." Messiaen placed his music on the piano and sat on the bench.

"When I was a younger I would visit my aunts who lived in the countryside at Fuligny in the Aube. The woods were full of birds. That's when I first began to take note of birds and their songs."

"Much of my life has largely been a waste of time!" Le Boulaire lamented.

"Time given to God is never wasted; God's eternity is charged with meaning."

"I have served in the military since 1934. Human existence has become a horror to me."

"Beauty is beyond horror," Messiaen said. "The human being is flesh and consciousness, body and soul; his heart is an abyss which can only be filled by the divine."

"There is nothing divine, and my heart's an abyss, that's for sure," Le Boulaire said with a smirk. "My heart's as cold as the snow and these damned howling winter winds."

"I don't believe it," Messiaen said, "You make the most beautiful of music."

"Surely you jest," Le Boulaire sneered. "I have a mind to quit the violin. I have never been recognized for my talents."

"I recognize them," Messiaen stated. "I am sure God does as well."

"Yes, well, you don't count. And God doesn't exist."

"Really?" Messiaen messed with the sleeves of his uniform.

"You live in another world."

"Thank you."

"*Thank you*, for what?"

"You have complimented me for my humility. I should be proud of that."

Le Boulaire raised his hands in disgust. "Our lives are in the shitter! How can you believe so easily while I cannot?" Le Boulaire squinted at Messiaen.

"I do not know," Messiaen said with a pause as he reflected upon the words of Thomas Aquinas: *to the believer, no explanation is necessary; to the unbeliever, no explanation is possible.*

*****

Meanwhile, Hauptmann Brüll had now arranged for Messiaen to take refuge in the priests' barracks to read in peace and quiet, and to have time for prayer and composing. Abbé Brossard welcomed his presence as well.

Messiaen began to develop the trio piece into the fourth movement, the *Intermède*.

Olivier Messiaen's proclivity to teaching could not be curtailed as he tried to explain the work to the Abbé.

"The second and seventh movements are related. Actually, the third movement came first when I was writing at Verdun. Parts of the second and fourth movements followed. I have already finished the fifth and eighth movements; both are songs of praise to Christ. I am still working on the sixth and seventh movements. In actuality, the most difficult piece may be the first movement. I have yet to compose it completely. However, I do know that there are birds in it."

The priest smiled lovingly. "Ah, yes, the birds. They are free and we are not. Feathered angels, are they not? Why, God himself is described as a bird several places in the sacred scriptures."

Messiaen nodded.

*****

Several days after the surprise visit by the Gestapo and SS, Messiaen smelled pipe smoke in his barracks. Lieutenant Busseron had come to pay a visit.

"Olivier, come with me. Le Boulaire, you too. Etienne Pasquier wants to meet you outside solitary confinement."

"Solitary confinement? The camp jail?"

"Yes. The Germans have a caged bird there and I want you to identify it by its song."

"This is strange," Messiaen smirked, following in the trace of Busseron's pipe smoke.

Several of the German guards looked at the men as they slogged their way through the snow and approached the solitary confinement hut.

Messiaen looked at Busseron and then Le Boulaire. "Now what?"

"Just listen. I'm sure the jailbird will begin playing – I mean singing."

The men were silent as they all listened. It started out low, but then the sound became more distinct. It was the sound of a clarinet.

"Henri!" Messiaen exclaimed loudly.

"It is!" Le Boulaire seemed equally as excited.

"*Oui*, it is our beloved Henri Akoka come back to haunt us," Busseron laughed.

"How in Heaven's name?" Messiaen asked Busseron with great incredulity. "We were told he was dead!"

"He is ingenious," Busseron drew more tobacco out of his pocket and began to fill the pipe's bowl. "It seems Henri was nearly at the Czechoslovakian border when he was recaptured. I was told that he played his clarinet for them, otherwise they would probably have shot him."

"Lucky bastard," Le Boulaire laughed.

"Not *so* lucky," Busseron replied with a nervous laugh, lighting his pipe again. "He has two weeks in the cooler."

As the men turned to leave, Busseron called out, "Akoka, we'll be here when you get out!"

"Not if I escape!" he answered back.

Then Messiaen heard Akoka begin playing his *Abime des Oiseaux*, Abyss of the Birds.

Akoka was playing it perfectly. Messiaen reflected on the abyss of time, in its sorrows and acedia. The birds offer a contrast, symbolizing the yearning for light, stars, rainbows and jubilant voices. How happy he was that Henri Akoka was alive!

*****

When Henri Akoka was eventually released from solitary confinement, he was surrounded by Pasquier, Le Boulaire, Messiaen, Busseron, Chevalier, and other prisoners in his barracks. He relished in telling and retelling of his escape and journey towards freedom.

"The actor, René Charles, a Polish prisoner, and I tunneled out," Akoka said in between puffs of his cigarette. "During the day we would hide and at night we'd walk. We walked over 550 damned kilometers in the snow, rain, sleet, and cold for seven nights only to be captured less than 20 kilometers from the Czechoslovakian border! I kept my clarinet with me and still had it in hand when I was captured. I played some melodies for the soldiers and I played some pieces for them, including the solo from the opera *Pré aux Clercs* by Ferdinand Hérold. It was surreal. As soon as I started playing, the soldiers relaxed and some even smiled. It was as if these men hadn't heard music for years. They soaked in every note I blew. Finally the German commander made me stop, but I was allowed to keep my clarinet! It is so unbelievable that I don't even believe it! I wouldn't believe it had it not happened to me!"

"Not so unbelievable" Messiaen broke in. "Music is next to prayer in its power to convert the hardened heart."

"You may be right," Akoka nodded before continuing with his story. "But the first thing Kommandant Bielas said to me upon my return was,

'You silly Jew, you are going to get yourself killed. And your love for the revolutionary Trotsky only makes it worse. You should be glad you are in Stalag 8A. Any other camp Kommandant would have you on a train bound for the work camp at Auschwitz.'"

After Akoka had finished telling his tale, the group dispersed leaving him alone with Messiaen.

"See," Messiaen argued, "it is God's will that you are here so that I can finish my quartet and you can play the clarinet. No one but you will be able to play the clarinet sections. I wrote them with you in mind beginning in Verdun. You know that."

"Well, it appears that God is on your side," Akoka smiled. "So finish the work so God can let me escape for good next time. I was almost free." His determination to survive and resolve to escape again was indomitable.

"We rehearse tonight at 1800 hours, as usual."

"*Merci*, Oli," Akoka smiled.

"In a way you and I both have cheated death," Messiaen said. "You thought I died in July and now here you are a veritable reanimated corpse. We heard stories that you were no more."

"Propaganda. We all survived. Unfortunately none of us made it to freedom."

"Thank God you are alive," Messiaen said, kissing Akoka on both cheeks. "We thought you were dead."

"I was alive," Akoka laughed. "Now I'm planning my next escape."

*****

Chapter 17

Solace

Olivier Messiaen was a very private person, yet many of the soldiers sought solace in his presence. His musician friends called him the composer-priest and even Abbé Brossard teased him that Messiaen heard more confessions than he did, though Messiaen could not grant absolution. Other prisoners treated him as a celebrity and found in his person some semblance of normality in light of the war and their imprisonment.

Whether they were intellectuals, musicians, artists, writers, or laborers, the imprisoned soldiers came — even if they had to wait outside the barracks in the cold and snow — to be inspired or experience whatever it was that made this man so different from his peers.

Messiaen was taken aback by the attention being given to him. Even some of the German soldiers and guards sought him out for a word of encouragement or advice in personal matters. In some ways he felt that the men desired the blessing of God as if he were a priest. There were many days when he fled to the priests' barracks where he could be alone to pray, read, and compose.

At night Messiaen slept with the rest of the prisoners in Barracks 19A. Jean Le Boulaire was in the next bunk and he was experiencing terrible flashbacks of the battlefield. One early morning Le Boulaire was experiencing a nightmare when Messiaen was awakened by his shouts.

"*Mon Dieu*! No more broken faces!" Le Boulaire cried out.

Messiaen got out of his bed and went over to Jean Le Boulaire's bedside. "Jean, it's Olivier. You're having a bad dream."

Le Boulaire was breathing rapidly and panted as he opened his eyes to behold the comfort of Messiaen.

"What happened?" asked Messiaen.

"All the soldiers! It was awful!" Jean quickly wiped away his tears.

"Everything is all right, Jean," Messiaen said, clasping his right hand with his.

"The women and children! The Germans killed them all!"

Henri Akoka stirred in the bunk below Le Boulaire.

"Don't let Henri wake up," Le Boulaire whispered. "I don't want him to see me like this."

"It's all right," Messiaen glanced below at Akoka. "He's asleep."

Le Boulaire explained how most all of his friends he had grown up with were war orphans as a result of the Great War in 1914-1918. His memory of that war was filled with images of all the maimed and gassed men who returned home. "All those broken faces and dismembered bodies! At night they come to haunt me! But now I have my own terrors of the savagery and barbarism of war! I saw despicable things and I did things I cannot forgive myself for doing. We committed the very things we sought to destroy! Oh, how I want to forget it all."

Messiaen closed his eyes and thought of his own father, wondering if his refusal to speak of the atrocities of the 1914-1918 war were for similar reasons. He briefly prayed for both Le Boulaire and his father.

"When we're dead and gone, what will be our legacy?" Le Boulaire asked, his eyes blinking back tears. "My reason rejects God — there is too much evil for there to be a good God."

"Suffering can take on a redemptive meaning," Messiaen's thoughts returned to the present. "All human life has meaning, no matter what the circumstances or condition — for all of life includes suffering, dying, and death. Christ came for all — believers and unbelievers alike."

"It is a pious thought, but must everything with you go back to God?" Le Boulaire asked in a whisper.

"Every subject can be a religious subject on condition that it is viewed through the eyes of one who believes."

"God is dead. We killed Him," Le Boulaire laughed to himself. "Or else he killed himself when he saw how vile, corrupt and loathsome human beings had become."

"He lives," Messiaen replied calmly but confidently.

"I don't believe. I refuse to believe." Le Boulaire was a silhouette among the shadows.

"Have you judged God?"

"Yes," Le Boulaire's tears subsided. "He is guilty of injustice and non-existence. So there! I see the Germans attending Mass in the chapel. They genuflect to the tabernacle just as you do. I know whose side the Church is on. It's on the side of power and prestige and control. Don't fool yourself."

"If a German Catholic is a Nazi," Messiaen argued, "then he has compromised his faith. But simply because a man genuflects does not mean he sees with the eyes of Christ."

"There is nothing in the tabernacle worth bending the knee for," Le Boulaire retorted as he wiped his nose. "It is medieval superstition, Monsieur. That's all it is. You are a kind man, but all your religion is simply pious talk."

"Christ humbled himself to become our daily bread."

"I've looked. I don't see it."

"We see what we want to see."

"Precisely. You want to see God and I do not. How can you love a god you cannot see?"

"He sees me."

"There," sighed Le Boulaire. "You did it again. It's moments like these that I am tempted to believe, tempted to pray again."

"Perhaps this is one temptation in which you should indulge." Messiaen said as he looked down and sighed. Outside the first bird of the morning began to chirp and sing.

"Olivier, you do not wear a mask," Le Boulaire cleared his throat. "You truly are who you seem to be."

"I would hope this is true," Messiaen nodded.

"That is what is so amazing. You really do believe all that you believe. You really do love."

"Yes, I love because God loves."

"Stop, please. God neither exists nor does he care for humans. And even if He did exist I would hate Him for acting like he cared."

Outside, the night began to give way to a glimmer of light.

"You do not hate God," Messiaen countered. "You hate what is not of God."

"Now I do not understand."

"You fear death."

"Don't *you?*" Le Boulaire looked at Messiaen askew.

"I do not fear death itself. Death is but our door to eternal life or eternal death. When I die I hope to breathe my last in a state of grace in this world and breathe in the fragrance of heaven. What will you say at the hour of death?"

"*Death?*"

"Yes. Death comes for us all."

"I prefer not to think of my death. That's morbid."

"Keeping death before our eyes does not mean we are obsessed with death; rather we are passionate about life. 'Number our days aright,' as the psalmist says."

"I hate death."

"So do I, but one must have the courage to look at what one hates in the face. Keep death ever before your eyes. That way you will live each day of your life, *non?*"

"You call this living?" Le Boulaire extended his arms, indicating their imprisonment.

"We cannot escape the cross."

"You are indeed a stranger to the world, Monsieur Messiaen."

"And I pray I am familiar to God."

More birds were now singing outdoors.

"When we recognize that no amount of earthly comfort and pleasure can completely satisfy our souls, then we are on our way to recognizing our need for God," said Messiaen.

"I shouldn't admit this, but I have been listening to you pray your rosary at night. Then you sing and chant to yourself in the wee hours of the morning. How can you sing in a world such as this?"

"I am alive!"

"So am I and I have nothing to sing about."

"Is there no song in your heart, Jean?" Messiaen asked sincerely as he continued standing next to Le Boulaire's bunk.

"Why would there be?" he sighed.

Messiaen took note of the first streak of dawn illuminating the window, his breath appearing and disappearing. Plato's allegory of the cave was true, yet it seemed that only Messiaen knew that the shadows on the cave walls were mere shadows; he'd been outside the cave and witnessed the light, the light of God.

"The sun has risen and the birds are singing," Messiaen said. "So should we! My faith is the great drama of my life. I believe therefore I sing!"

"I admire and respect your appreciation for life and your Christian charity, but your faith means nothing to me. Please keep your doctrine to yourself." Le Boulaire rolled over in his bunk, his back towards Messiaen.

"We are surrounded by innumerable and unexplainable events that reveal an invisible power, greater than ourselves to whom we must bow. God reveals Himself through His creation, whether in the song of a bird or a friendship! For me all things point to God."

"For me, nothing points to God," muttered Le Boulaire.

Messiaen looked at Le Boulaire and put his arm around him.

Le Boulaire wept silently. After a few minutes, Le Boulaire turned to face Messiaen and spoke again. "The gift of your music, your childlike love for birds and their songs, and your genuine kindness cause me to doubt my doubts. And I hate you for it.

"But I cannot hate you. I love you as do almost all the other men here. You truly are a gracious man. And in your faith I see the possibility for consolation. You are a man of God and yet I do not believe in God. You are an ambassador of Christ, and yet I do not believe in Christ. Yet it is in moments such as this that I am flooded with love and grace and want to cry out to God and ask for the gift of faith, the Holy Trinity, the Mass, all the Sacred Mysteries, the Death and Resurrection of Christ, and His Kingdom! You have caused me to stumble upon the question of the divine!" He stared at the ceiling and covered his eyes, shaking his head in confusion.

"I don't understand you and that poses a question for me," Le Boulaire continued, his eyes still covered. "Should I attribute it to your profound consciousness? But then I collapse back into reality and admit that it is all false. My life experience points me otherwise." Le Boulaire removed his hands from his face and turned to Messiaen.

"Christ came to suffer with us!" Messiaen exclaimed, a ray of sunlight gracing his face. "Just as there is a suffering even in our joy, so there is joy in our sufferings. Christ came to redeem all. He loves you."

"There, you did it again. I'm going back to sleep; perhaps I shall awaken only to discover that this has all been a horrible nightmare." He turned over in his bunk signaling the end of their theological discourse.

Life without God would be a nightmare, Messiaen said to himself as he returned to his bunk. *Life without God is incomprehensible. Without God there is no life. And without life there is nothing.*

The thought of life without God seemed as cold as the bitter winter which had descended upon eastern Germany.

He fingered his rosary beads, contemplating his predicament and praying for his colleagues. He longed to help Jean Le Boulaire understand the simplicity of faith but realized that Thomas Aquinas was correct in his assessment: *to the unbeliever, no explanation is possible.* Yet the words of the Apostle Paul offered some solace. *At present we see indistinctly as in a glass darkly, but then face to face.*

*****

"Music serves for us
as a conduit to the ineffable."
- Olivier Messiaen

Chapter 18

Incarnatus Est

December 1940

By December there was over 20 centimeters of snow on the ground and the freezing temperatures were unbearable. On Saint Nicholas' Day, Brüll arranged for Messiaen to use an empty room in the chapel barracks where he could read and compose in peace as well as rehearse with the other members of the quartet. "Consider it a Saint Nicholas Day gift," Brüll said.

"Thank you, Karl," Messiaen replied with a grin.

"As a Catholic lawyer I know that Saint Nicholas is also the patron saint of prisoners, wrongly condemned. He had a strong concern for justice. There is a story during Constantine's reign: three innocent men were once condemned but Nicholas interceded for them to the emperor who released them. In my case I have four men I'd like to see released."

Brüll placed his right hand on Messiaen's left shoulder.

By winter, Stalag 8A – far from being a holiday from the war – had become a home for the prisoners, though Messiaen longed for the embrace of his wife and the sight of young Pascal.

With its stage, Barracks 27 became a most popular place on Saturday nights for the men to divert their attention from the war and their situation. Over 400 men seated on wooden benches enjoyed songs and dance, comedians, musicians and storytellers from six in the evening until the nine o'clock curfew. But the evening hour from six to seven was reserved for the musicians performing classical music.

Pasquier told a group of men that were assembling a little before six, "If you don't like classical music, then don't come till seven."

"Any music will do; we're going stir crazy," Jacques Chevalier said. "We'll be there."

Messiaen was amazed that the barracks was almost always filled to capacity for the Saturday evening concerts. What wonders Bach, Mozart, Beethoven, Brahms, and Tchaikovsky worked in the midst of such primitive conditions. One soldier even broke down into tears as Messiaen performed his Preludes.

Even some of the German soldiers, officers, and guards were attending the performances. Several of the Germans would periodically come into the barracks while the men were rehearsing. Many of the Germans respected the members of the quartet. Hauptmann Karl Albert Brüll was a regular attendee of both the rehearsals and performances.

While the winds howled unceasingly and drifting snow blew through the timbers of the barracks, there was no escape from the icy dagger of winter's blade. As the weather worsened with more and more snow and the average temperature of $-25°$ Celsius, the prisoners were freezing. However, for the members of the quartet, Brüll kept wood in their stove so they were able to keep warm as they practiced. The men were unsure how to thank this kind German who seemed to have adopted the four players as his own sons.

As Messiaen prayed in the chapel, he rubbed his red, chafed hands together and blew on them for warmth. Reading the scripture, he kept returning to the Book of the Apocalypse. It was the book of the Bible that rekindled his desire to compose again. He had written a lecture which he gave to several priests and some prisoners entitled: *Colors and Numbers in the Apocalypse.*

He perused his notes: *Organ music symbolizes and makes real the contact between the mundane and the eternal. Indeed it makes a sacrament of the entire world. Music for me is an unknown fragrance, an unsleeping bird, music of stained glass church windows, a whirl of complementary colors, a theological rainbow.*

The angel of the tenth chapter of the Apocalypse is frightening, yet he thrills us with his color and message.

Messiaen wondered why he had been blessed with such a view that enabled him to continue believing in goodness while many of the other men believed the world was collapsing into the abyss. His unwavering faith in the face of the bleakness of war inspired many around him, yet even he had his moments of doubt. His prayer became more fervent as he beseeched the Lord for the grace of perseverance and an end to Hitler's tyranny.

One thing was for certain: now that the musicians all had instruments, Messiaen hardly had time to engage in any self-pity. He had a quartet to compose and, barring another escape by Henri Akoka, he was determined to premiere the work after Christmas.

The passion Messiaen felt for his quartet, now entitled *The Quartet for the End of Time*, consumed him. He slept very little and Brüll allowed him to compose at night while the other prisoners were asleep.

During the day, he was very demanding of his three musicians. Every evening and almost all afternoon on Saturdays he rehearsed the work with Pasquier, Akoka, and Le Boulaire in the makeshift concert hall.

At the piano he whistled a bird song. "This is a nightingale," he told them. Then he whistled again. "This is a song thrush. Don't you hear them?" The men all agreed even though they were unsure of what he was even talking about. Messiaen then began to sing to himself the notes, running his right hand through his hair, massaging his scalp with the fingers.

As for the Quartet, the men argued about musical technique and interpretation of the work as they labored to perfect it.

"What exactly are you doing with this piece?" Le Boulaire asked as he wrestled to come to comprehend Messiaen's musical genius.

"Time will tell," Messiaen tittered at his musical joke.

"There is no time in much of it," Le Boulaire held up his bow in his right hand and his violin in his left.

"Precisely. Nonetheless, Henri has the sense of the clarinet piece," Messiaen nodded to Henri Akoka who was playing his clarinet. "But hold this note till you cannot blow anymore," Messiaen said, pointing to the note on the musical score.

"When you can hold that note for as long as I can hold it, then hold it even longer!"

Akoka shook his head as he returned the clarinet to his lips.

"I am a pianist," Messiaen said. "And I am the composer. Indulge my request."

"*Merci*," Akoka said, pulling the instrument from his lips, "but do you realize how difficult this is to play without time signatures?!"

"Yes, that is why I wrote it," Messiaen smiled wryly from behind the piano. "If it were easy I would not ask you to play it."

"But, of course," Akoka rolled his eyes as he adjusted the clarinet's mouthpiece.

"Etienne," Messiaen turned to Corporal Pasquier holding his cello, "slower on the cello tempo in the fifth movement."

"Slower?" he said, pulling the bow off the strings. "*Mon Dieu!* Any slower and I won't be making any noise!"

"I want it slower — even slower."

"It's impossible to play that slow," Pasquier laughed aloud as he pleaded with Messiaen.

"You can," Messiaen assured him. "You can!"

"I *cannot* sustain the bow at that tempo," Pasquier said as he took out a cigarette and put it between his lips.

"You can do it," Messiaen said as he removed his glasses from his face, pinching the bridge of his nose and closing his eyes. "I believe in you. I believe in the music."

Henri Akoka reached over with his lighter and lit Pasquier's cigarette.

Messiaen replaced his glasses, slowly pushing them up his nose. He arranged the music sheets on the piano then turned to Jean Le Boulaire.

"Now Jean, let's work on the eighth movement. And remember, the tempo for the violin is inhumanly slow."

"And so is my ability to play it!" Le Boulaire cried out as he adjusted the strings, placed the instrument under his chin, and positioned his bow on the strings as he waited for Messiaen to begin the movement. "Inhumane!" he said, feigning anger.

Messiaen tapped the piano keys, striking the chord, and Le Boulaire slowly drew the bow across the strings.

"I need to hear you leaving the earth and ascending into heaven to God," Messiaen called out about halfway into the piece, as the instruments climaxed in the works' most dramatic movement. "A calming superiority – greater than silence, greater than silence!" Messiaen paused and listened as Le Boulaire played.

"Higher, higher!" Messiaen raised his voice enthusiastically again. "Sustain it! Keep it hanging there, floating heavenward!"

Pasquier's cigarette burned away as it dangled off his lips while both he and Akoka sat in rapt attention as Messiaen and Le Boulaire seemed to be engaged in a musical ecstasy. The repetitious chords and off-key dissonance of the piano notes intertwined with the haunting violin strings of the sublime ascending melody, like two lovers engaged in a passionate act of seasoned love.

Messiaen focused on the keyboard and lowered his head as the highest strands of notes from Le Boulaire's violin strings evaporated into the ethereal sky painted by the timeless Quartet.

As Le Boulaire lowered his violin, none of the men said anything in the transformed frosty air.

"Bravo!" Messiaen finally proclaimed, as he stood from the piano bench, breaking the reverent silence, "Jean Le Boulaire, you own that movement! Superbly played!"

"*Merci, beaucoup*," Le Boulaire tipped his hat to Messiaen.

"Now, what about you two?" Messiaen asked Pasquier and Akoka. "What are your thoughts, feelings, impressions?"

"Difficult to read, difficult to play, and especially difficult to play together," Pasquier lamented, with a smile.

"I know, I wrote it that way," Messiaen laughed. "But think of the beauty of it. I have liberated you from the prison of meter and rhythm. Music will never be the same. I have eliminated conventional musical expectations."

"*All* expectations," Akoka whispered, laughing.

"I heard that." Messiaen smiled as he tapped his music sheets, straightening them in a pile. "Henri, how are you coming along in maintaining the breath support for the long phrases and protracted crescendi in the third movement?

"I almost have it, but as for the extreme pianissimos in the altissimo register," Akoka said, paging through the score, "it can't be done."

"Oh, but it can, and you will do it. I know you can. I have faith in you."

"It's impossible!" Akoka argued.

"But you're doing it! Can't you hear?" Messiaen's eyes met Akoka's. "You're getting there."

Akoka groaned.

"Why do you doubt yourself? You can. You will. You must!"

Akoka rested his clarinet on his knees and shook his head.

"Etienne," Messiaen turned toward Pasquier. "How do you feel about the cello sections?"

"Never have such things been asked of a cellist before," Pasquier replied, removing his beret from his head.

"Well, now they have, haven't they?" Messiaen winked at him.

"The swift leaps from the high register to the low, and the harmonics!" Pasquier exclaimed. "They are very difficult to do!"

"Your point?" Messiaen's brow furrowed.

"You want daunting fortissimos and apocalyptic effects, but you also want unthinkably subtle ones," Pasquier said with incredulity, as he replaced his beret firmly on his head. "And the rhythms have to be absolutely precise!"

"In the final analysis," Messiaen explained quietly, "this piece of music is not about you, or me, or Jean, or Henri. It's about all of us — every man in this camp. Remember that. If we execute this work well, we may allow some poor souls to transcend their condition, even for a little while."

*****

Chapter 19

The End of Time

Messiaen, exhausted from the cold and from a long rehearsal, fell asleep early one evening before lights out. Sometime during the night he was awakened by a spirited discussion between Henri Akoka and Jean Le Boulaire.

Just as Messiaen was about to roll over and ask the men what they were talking about he heard his name mentioned.

"His music is marked by the dichotomy of dissonance and silence," Le Boulaire said, though Messiaen couldn't see him in the dark barracks. "He is a hard man to understand. He is both a mystic and a man. His love of birds and nature and musical melody is matched by his penchant for the severe, jolting noises."

"I agree," Akoka said, exhaling cigarette smoke, the glow from his cigarette casting an orange glow upon his ruddy face. "Where there is no harmony among the severity, a song will suddenly arise, such as the violin and piano in the eighth movement of the Quartet."

"I am an atheist and he knows this," Le Boulaire sighed, "but when he speaks or I observe him, I am tempted to believe."

Messiaen said nothing as he lay in his bunk listening to the men discuss his influence upon them.

"He has no idea how lucky he is to have been recognized by the conservatory," Le Boulaire lamented. "I, on the other hand, was completely overlooked. Yes, I have been ignored by the musical world — except for Olivier. I respect Messiaen. There is a mystery about him, one that I will always carry with me."

"'Elusive Olivier,' Pasquier calls him," Akoka said, taking yet another smoke from his cigarette.

"He does live in his own personal sphere," Le Boulaire said.

"Indeed," Akoka chuckled.

"That's why I admire him," Le Boulaire sighed.

"Perhaps one day people will ask us if we knew him when...." Akoka reflected.

"For all the rest of us who are demoralized by this damned war, Messiaen is strangely at peace," Le Boulaire said.

"He has more patience than Job," Akoka laughed. "While the world is staggering toward self-destruction, he's thinking thoughts of God, goodness, joy, forgiveness, and peace."

"Maybe he's right," Le Boulaire said. "Maybe God does exist. I don't know what to believe. I am a man who does not believe in God at all," Le Boulaire admitted. "Yet when I hear his music, I think that it all may be possible. Might there be something beyond ourselves? Then he'll begin to sing. That's what makes me stumble over the question of the divine. When I come upon a man like Messiaen, I cannot understand it, and that poses a great question mark for me. Perhaps I shall attribute it to his profound consciousness. But then I think again and look at the state of man on earth and this damned war and think that if there was a God, he would not permit this to happen. And my whole theory collapses in upon itself and I am left alone once again to ponder my meaning and place in the universe."

"I understand," Akoka said, putting his cigarette out in his tin ashtray. "He is certainly a different kind of man."

"As difficult to understand as his music," Le Boulaire proffered with a sigh and a slight chuckle.

The men then grew quiet and when all was silent, Messiaen returned to sleep, smiling to himself.

*****

At the next rehearsal, the men kept warm by standing near the iron stove in the center of the barracks. They began to discuss the Quartet and its lack of time signatures.

"What did you mean when you said your music could banish the temporal?" Le Boulaire asked Messiaen while tuning the strings of his violin.

"By eliminating conventional rhythm and meter," he answered, breathing into his cupped hands. "I will banish the temporal, and unleash a musical apocalypse whereby the central structure of composition – namely time – will be rendered irrelevant. In studying rhythm one studies Time; Time is measured and divided in a thousand ways, of which the most immediate for us is a continuous conversion or alteration of the future into the past. Yet Time is a created reality; it is the starting point for all of creation. In eternity, Time is not. There is no time in eternity."

The men looked at Messiaen, each one silently hoping that he wouldn't ask for an explanation of his treatise on time and eternity.

"One has to believe in the music," Messiaen began again. "In Heaven everything is sung. Therefore we cannot lose hope. We hope for what we do not see, and hope does not disappoint for we believe in the seen and the unseen."

Messiaen smiled and returned to his explanation of the Quartet. "When the angel declares 'there will be no more Time' I interpret him to mean that there will be no more space, no more time. One will leave the human dimension to rejoin eternity, where Christ will be all and will be in all. Eternity is not a long period of time; it is no time at all.

"My desire is to eliminate conventional notions of musical time, of past and future."

"The sixth movement is very different and difficult," Le Boulaire said, putting down his violin.

"The sixth movement of the quartet is marked in non-retrogradable rhythms—musical palindromes. There is a pianissimo in the middle of the movement and the tempo accelerates into a furious stringendo with a fortissimo theme and changes of register."

"Exactly what are we playing?" Le Boulaire asked as he placed his violin under his chin, examining the strings.

"Non-retrogradable rhythms," Messiaen answered. "The musical equivalent of the cessation of time, a musical metaphor, if you please."

"You and your metaphors," Le Boulaire laughed.

"It is a metaphor for the religious and philosophical idea of eternity," Messiaen explained. "The special rhythms are independent of the meter, and as such they contribute to the effect of banishing the temporal."

"Such slow tempi," Pasquier groaned teasingly.

"I have banished the temporal," Messiaen continued to lecture, speaking as much with his hands as his voice. "Time is a linear concept, dependent on forward motion and development, yet are not temporal dependency and time constraints human concepts, dependent upon our corporeal existence? It is true that music has a beginning, middle, and an end. It moves forward in time, forward in creation. But I am attempting to elude time by employing non-retrogradable rhythms and palindromes and birdsong. These non-retrogradable rhythms read the same in both direction, which has an effect of negating forward motion and temporal development in music, melody or song." Messiaen paced back and forth in front of the men, his hands still alive with movement; his glasses had slipped down his nose.

"The symmetry of palindromes achieves the same end by having the point of departure and point of arrival similar, linear forward motion and temporal development are denied, are reversed. These unequal patterns of chords and rhythms in a way revolve around each other, and by eliminating metrically defined phrases and avoiding beats, the effect is no meter, hence music devoid of time" Messiaen pressed his glasses to his face with his index finger and smiled. "Delightfully seditious, is it not? Musically rebellious and revolutionary, in fact."

"I told you that you were a revolutionary," Akoka said with a slight bow of his bead.

"Whatever you say," Pasquier laughed, seated with his cello between his legs and his bow in his right hand.

"Who would have known that our daily communicant leaned towards Trotsky?" Akoka laughed, carefully checking each of the pads and the joints of his clarinet.

"I never said that," Messiaen turned and frowned. "I am not that kind of revolutionary."

"Is there any significance in the fact that there are eight movements?" Pasquier asked, tuning the strings of his cello, his bow across the strings.

"*Oui*, why are there eight movements?" Akoka asked. "Shouldn't it be seven if it is all about the apocalypse and heaven?"

"Even though seven is the perfect number, Creation taking place in six days and then sanctified by the divine Sabbath. The seventh day of this repose extends into eternity and becomes the eighth day of eternal light, of unalterable peace. The musical octave — with seven intervals — symbolizes perfection, as in the seven days of creation, and the eighth day being the Day of the Lord.

"My inspiration to write music and compose is rooted in my Catholic faith and as a believer. My faith is everything. Saint Paul once wrote, 'Woe to me if I do not preach the gospel.' I understand his predicament. My cry is similar: Woe to me if I do not compose. For you see, I am a believing musician. As such I am free." Messiaen placed his left hand over his heart and raised his right to heaven.

"The Eternal penetrates the temporal — the Paschal Mystery is relived in the Liturgy and in our own lives. There is a dance of death and life, a constant conflict between death and life, yet there is an eternal serenity amid such apocalyptic dissonance.

"There is always hope — even in the darkest night."

*****

Chapter 20

Hope

The men were restless as Christmas approached.

"Play the La Marseilles! They can't put us all in solitary!" some of the French soldiers cried out at one of the Saturday evening concerts. Messiaen nodded at the piano and the three other musicians began playing variations on the theme.

The French, Belgian, and British soldiers went wild stamping their feet and began singing along until one of the guards caught the melody.

"*Nein, nein,*" he yelled, "*Musiker!* Not that song! You, musician," he said, pointing his rifle at Messiaen. "Stop that!"

The men went back to playing French Christmas carols and the men sang along – even some of the German guards.

Back in the barracks, the men discussed the unfortunate turn of events related to the war on Britain. All through September, October and November London had been bombed. Even now as Christmas approached the German offensive was unrelenting.

When the Germans were out of earshot, the soldiers were animated in their opinions.

"Bombing London at night for over a hundred nights straight!" Sergeant Chevalier thundered. "Bombing civilian targets! The Nazis will stop at nothing! Now thousands and thousands of Londoners are dead!"

"Over 30,000 at last count." Lieutenant Busseron said coldly, his eyes cast down as he slowly puffed on his pipe, the smoke encircling his face.

"Nazi bastards!" One of the men said, cursing as well.

Messiaen was convinced that war was ridiculous, decided by madmen in war rooms, miles away from any battlefield or prison camp.

"Where the hell are the Americans?" Chevalier asked aloud. "What will it take to convince them to come to our aid?"

"Their economy is built on big business and big business has an ally in German industry," Busseron said as he removed his pipe from his mouth.

"But what if the Germans were killing American civilians?" Chevalier asked with rhetorical flourish.

"They have," Busseron explained, working to relight his pipe. "The Germans have torpedoed and sunk several American ships, killing crew members, but the U.S. has so far stayed out of the war. However, the U.S. is not neutral. It's complicated" Busseron continued with a sigh as he fumbled with his pipe. "The only way the Americans will get into the war is if some of their soldiers are killed. Then they'll come up swinging. The Americans are an interesting lot, quite fickle unless they are directly affected by war. Mark my word. You watch. They did nothing during *Kristallnacht*. Their government merely recalled their ambassador, but it was business as usual. Presently, the majority of Americans are either blind or indifferent to the plight of the rest of the world."

*****

On Christmas Eve as Messiaen was preparing to attend Mass, he saw Jean Le Boulaire lying in his bunk.

"Come to Mass with me," Messiaen said to him.

"I don't go to church," Le Boulaire opened his eyes and wiped the sleep away. "You know that."

Messiaen furrowed his brows and looked intently at his friend. "I do know that. But I also know that it will lift your soul."

"It's the twentieth century, Olivier. I'm not religious. You are. *Joyeux Noel*. Now I'm going back to sleep."

"*Tres bien*. Happy Christmas to you too. The Germans are serving coffee and baked bread with *fromage blanc* after Mass."

"Now that's worth getting out of bed for," Le Boulaire's demeanor changed as he opened his eyes wide and smiled.

In the chapel, Midnight Mass was attended by German and French soldiers alike. It seemed as though, just for the night, everyone seemed to forget the war – except for the fact that the French were not free. The

Germans soldiers, though familiar to the French soldiers, were despised because they were keeping the Frenchmen from their families and loved ones. Nevertheless, the Germans were not free either, trapped in an insidious war.

One of the French soldiers, upon entering the chapel and seeing Germans kneeling alongside their French prisoners asked, "Isn't this behavior called fraternizing with the enemy?"

"It's Christmas," came a French voice. It was Abbé Brossard. His ruddy face matched his commitment to every man under his charge, regardless of what uniform he wore.

"So what of the suffering we experience here?" Abbé Brossard asked the men. "Christ came to suffer with us! There is joy in our sufferings. Christ came to redeem all – French and German alike."

During Mass, Messiaen could hear the church bells ringing in the town of Görlitz and the Polish town across the river. Silence reigned as he basked in the familiar sounds of church bells with the knowledge that Christmas still came despite the inhumanity of war and oppression.

After Mass, the men were welcomed to the mess hall where coffee and pastries, cheese, and cake was served. There were more men in the mess hall than had been in the chapel.

"What I wouldn't give for some real coffee," Sergeant Jacques Chevalier lamented, stumbling through the door, running his hand through his tousled hair. He poured himself a cup of ersatz coffee.

"This shit is worse than piss," Busseron smirked as he sipped some of the drink.

"It is piss," Chevalier laughed as he spat the drink back in the cup.

"Well, then, I stand corrected," Busseron nodded, taking another sip of the ersatz coffee. "Piss is better."

"What I wouldn't give for a loaf of freshly baked bread and a bottle of red wine," Pasquier said, suddenly appearing in the hall with Jean Le Boulaire.

"*Oui*, you and the entire camp, old man." Messiaen patted Pasquier on the back.

*****

In the two weeks following Christmas, the musicians labored intensively over the quartet as they were given orders of sorts that the work was to premiere on Wednesday evening, 15 January, with German officers in attendance. Messiaen was uncertain why there was so much attention being showered upon his creation.

The Kommandant had even given orders that tickets were to be printed and that the only entertainment scheduled for that night was to be Messiaen's *Quator pour la Fin du Temps* performed by the four musicians.

Brüll bought Pasquier and Le Boulaire rosin and strings for the cello and violin, while he gave Akoka several new reeds for his clarinet.

Messiaen was well aware that part of the German strategy in keeping a good image in the French press was not only for the camps to entertain both Germans and French alike with concerts, but they wanted the world to see how cultural the Nazis could be.

*****

The final rehearsals were the most intense, yet the best. The four men, from varied backgrounds and worldviews, had bonded and congealed, amalgamating to become *the Quartet for the End of Time*.

Messiaen explained that timbre was just as important as pitch and time as he stared out the frosted window pane. "As a young student at the Paris Conservatoire I went to *Sainte-Chapelle* in Paris. I recall seeing the stained glass windows for the first time. It was a shining revelation, which I've never forgotten, and this first impression as a child—I was ten years old at the time—became a key experience for my later musical thinking. When I hear music, I see color."

He then turned to the three musicians, his left hand and fingers caressing his forehead.

"Of the first movement, *Crystal Liturgy*, what do you think? Jean Le Boulaire, You are my nightingale. Henri Akoka, you are my blackbird. The birdsongs represent the harmonious silence of heaven as they celebrate with song the dawn from on high. You know," Messiaen pondered, "it is probable that in the artistic hierarchy, birds are the greatest musicians on our planet. And they do not sing or call according to meter or rhythm. So why should I feel compelled to enslave my music to meter and rhythm?" Messiaen examined the faces of his fellow musicians as he continued to lecture.

"In *Abyss of the Birds*, the third movement, Henri's clarinet solo, the abyss is Time, with its dreariness and gloom. The clarinet begins in sadness with sustained swelling sounds: *pianissimo*, *crescendo molto*, and to the most excruciating *fortissimo*. The song is in the style of the blackbird. The birds are the opposite of Time: they represent our longing for light, for stars, for rainbows, and for jubilant song!" Messiaen was nearly singing his words as he described the work, his face bright with joy and body animated as if he were a marionette on strings.

"Above the abyss the birds joyfully fly free. And every man in the theatre who hears this movement will be freed, even if for only less than an hour. The return to desolation is manifested in the dark timbre of the clarinet's lower register."

Pasquier and Le Boulaire rosined their bows and tuned their strings. Akoka was still struggling with his clarinet piece.

"Henri, you have captured the horror of the abyss in your ability to hold the notes for as long as you can. The notes are symbolic of eternity – in all its horror of the abyss." He grew silent as the men listened intently.

"As humans make war; the birds sing!" he began speaking again. "The bird is a symbol of freedom. We walk; he flies. We drop bombs; he sings. I doubt that one can find in any human music, however inspired, melodies and rhythms that have the sovereign freedom of birdsong."

Messiaen paused in thought as he considered how elusive human freedom had become; just as injured birds long to fly, detained human beings were fascinated with the flight of birds.

The three musicians observed Messiaen as he disappeared into his own world of thought and prayer.

Messiaen contemplated human freedom, he realized that it was a gift that he and the others had often taken for granted, but now that it had been deprived them, they were consumed with the desire for it, haunted by its memory.

> *In the beginning was the Word, and the Word was with God, and the Word was God. He was in the beginning with God. All things came to be through him, and without him nothing came to be. What came to be through him was life, and this life was the light of the human race; the light shines in the darkness, and the darkness has not overcome it.*
>
> *The true light, which enlightens everyone, was coming into the world. And the Word became flesh and made his dwelling among us, and we saw his glory, the glory as of the Father's only Son, full of grace and truth (Jn 1: 1-5, 9, 14).*
>
> *The Word became flesh and dwelt among us.*

Here they were: a delirious composer with technically demanding music in frigid conditions; starving artists with frozen fingertips and old, weathered, warped instruments. If they were to execute the debut of Messiaen's piece with any degree of precision, then it would be nothing shy of a miracle.

*****

"This was a great act of faith."

Olivier Messiaen,
referring to the *Quator pour la Fin du Temps.*

Chapter 21

The Quartet

January 1941

By the first week of 1941, another snowstorm had pummeled the region, blowing and drifting, making the total snow on the ground more than 50 centimeters. The temperatures plunged to the extremes. The roofs of all the barracks were covered in snow and every window was frosted over.

Now, after months of composing, rehearsing, adjusting and polishing the Quartet, Messiaen was prepared to premiere the piece, albeit on broken and dilapidated instruments with the added concern of frostbite threatening the musicians' fingers and toes.

The prisoners began gathering in the theatre barracks around an hour before the performance was scheduled, even those who had never listened to chamber music before. By seven o'clock all the seats were taken, about four hundred in all – not including the German officers, soldiers, and guards who were also in attendance.

The men were so cold they didn't care how they looked. Some were wearing colorful mufflers their mothers, sisters, girlfriends, or wives had sent them. They wore various rags and coats, shoes and boots to keep their feet warm. What a rag-tag appearance these men displayed. Yet they were there to participate in a premiere of the music of the French composer, Olivier Messiaen.

Kommandant Bielas had gone to the trouble of having one of the artist-inmates draw a cover in Art Nouveau style for the programs that were printed for the musical debut. The title of the composition appeared on the cover, with Messiaen's name listed as the composer and pianist while the names of Akoka, Pasquier, and Le Boulaire appeared as the members of the quartet. The camp's official stamp of Stalag VIIIA Görlitz appeared on the top left of the program, indicating that the performance was officially approved by the Wehrmacht.

So much did the Kommandant approve of the performance that he had invited other German officers to attend the premiere, and even permitted quarantined prisoners to attend. Several wounded men from the infirmary were wheeled in on stretchers and wheelchairs to hear the work. All were packed into the unheated Barracks 27 for the music of Messiaen.

Despite the charged atmosphere of a musical premiere, the German eagles and swastikas — "the broken cross" — reminded the assembled of their situation and the ongoing war.

Abbé Jean Brossard was also in attendance. His eyes were not as tired this evening, his hair was neatly combed and his cassock was freshly washed and pressed. His face was clean shaven, yet the shadow of his beard remained.

Pasquier laughed at how the members of the quartet were dressed. He and Messiaen were clothed in patched bottle green Czechoslovakian uniforms, badly torn. They all wore their military berets. All four performers were wearing two pairs of socks and wooden clogs because of the extreme chill and draft.

The men prepared to perform in front of priests, peasants, factory laborers, intellectuals, medics, doctors, lawyers, reluctant draftees, and French, Polish, British, and Belgian career soldiers. The kingdom of God was well represented. As far as the music was concerned, Henri Akoka joked that they were all lost regarding Messiaen's music — except for Messiaen.

As Messiaen stepped forward to address the crowd concerning the musical composition that they were about to hear, the assembly quieted itself. Messiaen awkwardly adjusted his glasses on his face, but when the timid composer spoke to the crowd, his countenance changed. He was no longer the quiet, reserved, hermit-monk composer, but the lecturer: alive, animated, self-confident as if introducing his first-born son. In his voice was the joy of his being able to share his composition with all; in his presence, newfound strength, vim, and vigor.

"The quartet you are about to hear is nearly an hour-long piece of eight movements for violin, cello, clarinet, and piano. My fortuitous choice of instrumentation for this quartet was made rather providentially since the four musicians you see before you all found themselves prisoners of war and ultimately sent here to Stalag 8A. Thanks to the cooperation of a few good German officers, we were able to secure the cello, violin, and piano." He motioned with his hand to Kommandant Bielas and Hauptmann Brüll. "Our dear Henri Akoka came to us already supplied with his clarinet. In fact, he goes everywhere with it."

Messiaen winked at Akoka and a few laughs were heard, the men obviously recalling Akoka's escape with the instrument and subsequent return to the camp with it still secure under his arm. "All in all, I wrote the composition with these four instruments in mind because they were the four instruments I had at hand.

"As for the piece of music itself, this quartet was written for the end of time," he continued, now pacing in front of the audience. "But this is not a play on words, nor a reference to the direction the war is going or our length of captivity. It does, however, convey the end of the notion of past and future in musical terms.

"It all began when I was reading the Book of the Apocalypse," he said as he clasped his hands together as if in prayer. "I was intrigued by the tenth chapter. It reads:

> *And I saw another mighty angel come down from heaven, clothed with a cloud: and a rainbow was upon his head, and his face was as it were the sun, and his feet as pillars of fire. In his hand he held a small scroll that had been opened. He then set his right foot upon the sea, and his left foot on the land.... Then the angel I saw standing on the sea and on the land raised his right hand to heaven and swore by the one who lives forever and ever, who created heaven and earth and sea and all that is in them, 'There shall be no more Time...'*

Messiaen broke off mid-sentence, touched his chin and held his position briefly, lost in thought, trying to remember what he was explaining. "The music of the future will have no time. The modes and rhythms of western music are impoverished. I use new modes, new rhythms, yet plainchant is so important. Religious matters include everything – God and His entire creation." Messiaen placed his thumb on the bridge of his glasses and slowly pushed them up his nose.

"I am a student of physics and astronomy as well as theology and music. God reveals Himself through His creation, whether in the immensity of a galaxy or the intricacies of an atom, or the song of a bird! Rainbows, stained glass, the planets. All things point to God. Even the aurora borealis contributed to the vision for this quartet. Since God is omnipresent, music dealing with theological subjects can and must be extremely varied."

By now there was conspicuous unease in the assemblage: restless coughs, the shuffling of feet and murmuring.

"The modes, realizing melodically and harmonically a sort of tonal ubiquity or omnipresence, bring the listener closer to infinity, to eternity in space. The special rhythms, independent of the meter, powerfully contribute to the effect of banishing the temporal.

"Some of you men may not be religious, but '*Je suis né croyant,*' I was born a believer. As a Catholic Christian, I expect the Resurrection of the Dead. This Quartet is an apocalypse in itself, an epiphany, an unveiling of something new, music *without* time performed *within* time." Messiaen glanced over at Abbé Brossard.

"Music is a gift, marked by time. But in musical terms, I do not wish to perpetuate musical time as mere drumbeats. Yet I tell you that the music of the future will have no time. Time is encounter. If time stands still we can fully encounter reality, and the greatest reality is God. T.S. Eliot wrote, 'There is a music heard so deeply that it isn't heard at all. You are the music while the music lasts.' Therefore, live in the present moment. Always." Messiaen paused to glance at the musicians behind him.

"Our vocation is to give God praise and glory. I do it through my music. The sound of music penetrates the stillness of silence. Prayer sanctifies our time. Keeping vigil in the darkness and celebrating lauds at sunrise. Joy transcends our temporal existence. We can even find joy in the pain and suffering."

Messiaen paused, removed his glasses out of habit, holding the lenses up to the light and examined the scratched lenses.

"Think of the stained glass windows of a church. The glass fills with light just as lauds are chanted. The joyful praise rises as the light crawls up the panes. We are like those shards of colored glass. In unity with all the other pieces in the panel, we reveal the image of Christ and his Church. Mid-afternoon to the vesper hour, the light begins to give way to shadows. The world is fading away; death comes for us all. Like a burning candle, so is a man living life fully."

He paused again, returned his glasses to his face, and looked at his audience with rapt attention. Those gathered were growing more restless, particularly Lieutenant Simon Busseron and Sergeant Jacques Chevalier.

"Yet there is joy even in this dank camp, for I refuse to embrace the darkness and the destructive chaos of war. I am called to create order where there is none. The dichotomy of the beauty of nature and the wanton turmoil of war is only temporary. Yes, everything is temporary. For me music is a sacrament, an encounter with the living God, and composition is often my most sincere prayer."

Le Boulaire cleared his throat, raising his bow and resting it on the music stand in front of him. Pasquier gave Messiaen a stern-faced nod as if to hurry Messiaen along with his lengthy dissertation.

"If by my music I can lift someone's soul then I have not lived in vain. Even among the alienated, war-torn, chaos-weary people, war does bring people together. Despair, sadness, grief, can give way to joy, faith, hope, charity. A song sung is never sad. It conveys hope." Messiaen smiled at his audience.

"The Paschal Mystery, the resurrected life, is not simply about heaven or life hereafter, but rather is about life now, living the life of Christ today, in the ordinariness of our daily existence. My quartet is not about apocalyptic catastrophes, but is about God's eternity piercing our own chronological existence. Oh, if we but had the eyes to see—"

Messiaen stopped mid-sentence and sighed, touching his throat as if holding down emotion, before continuing with his explanation of the quartet.

"The *Quartet for the End of Time* comprises eight movements and includes early-morning bird calls, the angel who announces the end of time, and Christ. The Quartet is born of religious imagery. Music is something greater than ourselves and our present existence. We will be free again someday."

The looks on the men's faces revealed befuddlement, perplexity, and intensity as they awaited the first notes of what they hoped would be a composition of historic proportions. All the attention that the Germans had allowed to build for the piece gave Messiaen a combination of both supreme confidence and great anxiety.

Etienne Pasquier caressed his cello and rosined his bow; Jean Le Boulaire prepared his violin, organizing the score on the music stand; Henri Akoka's clarinet rested on his knees as he smiled at all those assembled — even the German officers and guards.

Messiaen continued with his introduction: "The first movement is entitled: *The Crystal Liturgy*. Between three and four in the morning, there is the awakening of birds: a solo blackbird or nightingale improvises, surrounded by a shimmer of sound, by a halo of trills lost very high in the trees. Transpose this onto a religious plane and you have the harmonious silence of Heaven." His eyes were focused above and his hands expressive.

"The second movement is entitled *Vocalise for the Angel Announcing the End of Time*: the first and third parts evoke the power of this strong angel, crowned with a rainbow and clothed in clouds, one foot on the sea and the other on land. The central section deals with the impalpable harmonies of heaven, the piano playing soft cascades of chords: blue and mauve, gold and green, red-violet, blue-orange; all of this dominated by steel-grey. These chords, faraway chimes, surround the plainchant-like melody of the violin and cello. Blue and orange clouds."

Messiaen stepped toward Akoka and nodded. "The third movement, which incidentally was the first movement composed, is entitled *Abyss of the Birds*. It is a clarinet solo. The abyss is Time with its sadness, its weariness. The birds are the opposite of Time; they are our desire for light, for stars, for rainbows, and for jubilant songs.

"The fourth movement is an Interlude. I simply call it *Scherzo*. It is of a more outgoing character than the other movements, but related to them nonetheless by various melodic references.

"The fifth movement is a louange, a song of praise. It is entitled, *Praise to the Eternity of Jesus.* It is an otherworldly string melody above the piano. It builds to a shimmering climax and then fades into ether. Jesus represents, in this context, the word of God. One long, extremely slow phrase by the cello glorifies with infinitely slow tenderness and reverence the eternity of this powerful and gentle Word. Majestically the melody unfolds like a distant memory, tender and all encompassing. For 'In the beginning was the Word, and the Word was with God, and the Word was God.'" Messiaen stepped back, looking at his notes on the piano before continuing his description of the piece. Sergeant Chevalier coughed intentionally and waved his hand in circles, motioning for Messiaen to simply get to the actual music.

"The sixth movement is the *Dance of Fury, for the Seven Trumpets,*" Messiaen continued, his voice louder, much to the chagrin of Chevalier who rolled his eyes and lowered his head. "Rhythmically, it is the most idiosyncratic movement of the quartet. The four instruments in unison give the effect of gongs and trumpets. The first six trumpets of the Apocalypse attend various catastrophes; the trumpet of the seventh angel announces the consummation of the mystery of God. It is music of stone, a formidable sonority; movement as irresistible as steel, as huge blocks of livid fury or ice-like frenzy. Listen particularly, toward the end of the piece, to the terrifying *fortissimo* of the theme in augmentation and with change of register of its different notes."

There were more pronounced impatient coughs and murmuring in the audience, yet Messiaen persevered.

"The seventh movement is entitled *Tangle of Rainbows, for the Angel Announcing the End of Time.* This movement is dedicated to the angel, and even more so, to the rainbow covering him. The rainbow symbolizes peace, wisdom, and all luminous and resonant vibration," he said, tracing a rainbow in the air with his right hand.

"In my colored dreams I hear and see ordered melodies and chords, familiar hues and forms; then, following this transitory stage I pass into the unreal and submit ecstatically to a vortex, a dizzying interpenetration of superhuman sounds and colors. These fiery swords, these rivers of blue-orange lava, these turbulent shooting stars: Behold the rainbows!"

Messiaen raised his hands upward, as if pointing to an actual rainbow above the barracks.

"Finally, the eighth and final movement is another louange entitled *Praise to the Immortality of Jesus.*" His voice softened. "It is an expansive violin solo similar to the fifth movement, but it is performed on the violin with rhythmic piano chords. The violin sings to highest heaven and evaporates into silence. Why this second louange?" He looked around at his audience, briefly wondering if any of the men before him would be able to provide an answer. After an adequate pause for a response that never came, he gave the answer.

"It addresses more specifically the second aspect of Jesus, Jesus the Man, the Word made flesh and raised from the dead and immortalized to make His life known to us. This movement is pure love. It ascends gradually toward an intense peak, the ascension of man towards God, of the Son of God toward his Father. It calls to mind our own journey as creature and being made divine in Paradise."

Messiaen looked closely at the audience, aware that he had explained far too much for the novice gathering. He joined his hands together and motioned to the other members of the quartet. "Therefore, without further adieu, and in homage to the Angel of the Apocalypse, who lifts his hand toward heaven, saying, 'There shall be no more Time,' I present to you the *Quartet for the End of Time.*"

There was scattered applause as Messiaen walked behind the piano and sat down. He secured his music, examined the keys, and nodded to Henri Akoka who intoned the first notes on his clarinet. He was soon followed by Messiaen on the piano, Pasquier on the cello, and lastly, Jean Le Boulaire on the violin.

The premiere was underway. Messiaen's image of birds flying over the abyss captured the essence of their quartet ransoming the souls of all the prisoners by means of the gift of his music. He prayed that by the performance of the quartet the mystery of God would be revealed.

*****

After nearly an hour of music, the performers were finished. The silence that followed the last strains of the violin was a music all its own. This silence was not simply an absence of sound, but an echo of timelessness – the innocence of silence – the very breath of God which spoke the world into existence. It was a virginal peace pregnant with possibility, where no one moved or seemingly breathed, for it appeared that no one wanted to break the spell that Messiaen's music had cast over his hearers.

The quartet had muted the strains of war with its sound and silence. It was indeed as if chronological time no longer mattered, and had been graced with, or rather, had pierced eternity.

An expectant silence prolonged the strain of the last note of the solo violin. Slowly the applause began, applause either commending the end of an incomprehensible work or surrendering their praise to the wonder of genius. Many of the men stood in ovation; others likely stood because they had been sitting for too long.

"Miraculous," Messiaen said to his companion performers. "*Merci beaucoup.*" All four men stepped forward and bowed to the audience.

"Perfect!" Pasquier said almost in a hushed whisper.

"Where were we for the past hour?" was all Le Boulaire could say, so overcome was he by emotion.

Akoka's mouth was half-open as he slowly formulated the words, "What a revelation."

"It was indeed a miracle," Messiaen said with firm conviction. "A musical epiphany. Never before have I been listened to with such attention and understanding. More than 400 men, many of whom have never listened to chamber music, and they listened with such a religious silence!" Messiaen reflected. "I have a feeling that for a brief time, all of us imprisoned by this war were set free. Music witnesses to the heart that we are all brothers.

"Blithe ecstasy, a glimpse of the beatific vision," Messiaen said, reflecting upon his study of Thomas Aquinas and the *Summa Theologiae*. He removed his rosary from his pocket, kissed the crucifix, and crossed himself.

The three musicians took Messiaen's program and each man signed it.

Pasquier wrote: "The camp of Görlitz...Barracks 27B, our theatre...outside, night, snow, misery...here, a miracle: the *Quator pour la Fin du Temps* – transports us to a wonderful Paradise, lifts us from this abominable earth. Thank you immensely, dear Olivier, poet of Eternal Purity."

Akoka wrote: "To Olivier Messiaen, who revealed Music to me. I try in vain by these few words to prove to him my gratitude but I doubt that I will ever be able to do so."

Le Boulaire wrote: "To Olivier Messiaen, my great friend, who with the Quartet for the End of Time made me take a grand and magnificent voyage to a wonderful world. A thousand thanks as well as my great admiration and friendship."

Messiaen found himself surrounded by many of the prisoners, totally uneducated concerning classical music, but quite taken by the experience of the quartet. Some came up to him to shake his hand or pat him on the back, while others vocally acknowledged his gift to them in their captivity.

One soldier who waited for the other soldiers to clear the barracks was Jacques Chevalier. He embraced Messiaen and wept on his shoulder.

"Professor Messiaen, I have not experienced such joy in many years. *Merci.*" With that, Chevalier could say no more and hurried out of the barracks, leaving Messiaen alone with his musicians.

He was so taken by the men's show of emotion that he himself wept, struck by the transfiguring power of his music and how it had transformed the banal Stalag into something sublime. Perhaps he wasn't so misunderstood after all.

Pasquier and Le Boulaire put their instruments away and left the barracks, clapping Messiaen on the shoulder on their way out.

"Never have I been as free," Messiaen said to Akoka, who was removing the reed from his clarinet. "Of all prisoners, I am the most free."

"You are delirious." Akoka smiled. "But the Quartet was indeed a musical triumph."

"I composed this quartet in order to escape from the snow, from the war, from captivity, and from myself," Messiaen said, rubbing his forehead as his thoughts turned to Claire and Pascal.

"Well, I think it worked," Henri smiled, lighting a cigarette. "Your music muted the war, at least for an hour."

"God's eternity is charged with meaning."

The warmth in Messiaen's heart thawed the icy numbness in his frozen toes, frigid hands, cold ears and runny nose. He laughed at himself, overjoyed that he had – even for a short time – halted the flow of time, though it was only an illusion.

Imagine me attempting to stop time, he chuckled to himself while at the point of tears.

Stalag VIII A
GÖRLITZ

PREMIÈRE AUDITION
DU
QVATVOR
DE LA FIN DU TEMPS
d'
Olivier Messiaen
15 Janvier 1941

exécuté par
Olivier MESSIAEN
Etienne PASQUIER
Jean LE BOULAIRE
Henri AKOKA

"Never before have I been listened to
with such attention and understanding."

- Olivier Messiaen
at the conclusion of the premiere of the Quartet

Chapter 22

Resurrexit

March 1941

A review appeared in the spring issue of *Lumignon*, the French-language camp newspaper, under the headline: *Première at the Camp*.

> *It was our good fortune to have witnessed in this camp the first performance of a masterpiece. And what's strange is that in a prison barracks we felt just the same tumultuous and partisan atmosphere of some premières: latent as much with passionate acclaim as with angry denunciation. And while there was fervent enthusiasm on some rows, it was impossible not to sense the irritation on others. Reminiscences of the time speak of a reaction like this when one evening in 1913 at the Théâtre des Champs-Elysées, Le Sacre du Printemps, The Rite of Spring, by Stravinsky, was first performed.*

> *It is often a mark of a work's greatness that it has provoked conflict on the occasion of its birth. The last note of Messiaen's Quator pour la Fin du Temps was followed by a moment of silence which established the sovereign mastery of the music.*

*****

A few weeks later, at one of the Saturday evening performances, several senior German officers came to the camp and attended one of the musical performances led by Messiaen. The Kommandant took Hauptmann Brüll aside. Messiaen observed the Germans as he and the others finished their performance of a work by Mozart, Faure's *Pavane* scored for piano, violin, cello, and clarinet by Messiaen, and Beethoven's

Trio for piano, clarinet and cello, but Messiaen had added a violin section for Le Boulaire, transforming it into a quartet, with due apologies to Ludwig.

After the German brass left and the performance had concluded, Brüll approached Messiaen and confided to him, "Next week certain French prisoners will be repatriated to France. Don't miss the train. It appears that the organist Marcel Dupré has written the German government asking for your release. Let the cellist and violinist and the clarinetist know; I may be able to have them released as well."

The next week Brüll came to the barracks and quietly informed Messiaen that he was to be repatriated since he had served as an orderly. Brüll then explained to Pasquier that he had falsified his prison record to show that Pasquier was unarmed when he was captured, despite the facts to the contrary. Brüll had forged Pasquier's repatriation form, indicating that he was an unarmed orderly when captured. However, any man who was a *Soldat-Musicien*, Soldier-Musician, was to be repatriated without question. For reasons beyond Brüll's control, the violinist, Jean Le Boulaire, was to remain incarcerated. The only musician among them who truly was a *soldat-musicien* was Henri Akoka. Kommandant Bielas then authorized Brüll to drive the three men to the train station in Görlitz.

There was not much time for farewells. Messiaen, Pasquier, and Akoka collected their few belongings and prepared to leave.

Right before Messiaen left his barracks, he was able to have a few minutes alone with Jean Le Boulaire, who was lying in his bunk with the pillow over his head.

"I so regret that your name has not made it to the list of musicians who will be repatriated," Messiaen said.

"Your God has once again ignored me, but heard your prayers."

"This is not true," Messiaen explained.

"Then how do you explain my being ignored as a musician?" he said removing the pillow and looking at Messiaen. "I am forever condemned to be a soldier. Yet you know that I detest the military life. This whole war disgusts me. Everything about war disgusts me. I am not the same man I was back in 1934 when I was first called up for active military duty."

"None of us is, Jean," Messiaen said.

"Of this I am sure. The only good memory, the only good thing to come out of this whole damned war was your Quartet. And the eighth movement. That eighth movement will never belong to anyone else but me," he sighed as his eyes glistened.

"It is yours," Messiaen nodded. "You brought the quartet to its finality. Your violin playing ascended to the heavens."

"*Oui. Merci.*" Boulaire smiled. "It's a jewel that will forever be with me. Musically speaking, it's the most beautiful thing that I have ever experienced in my life. It is likely the most beautiful thing I have ever done in my entire life!"

The two men embraced as brothers and Le Boulaire kissed Messiaen on the cheek. "Pray for me."

"The Lord has heard your prayers. He is merely delayed in answering them."

"Then have him hurry."

Messiaen exited the barracks for the last time. Brüll ushered Henri Akoka, Etienne Pasquier, and Olivier Messiaen past the warning lines, past the guard dogs, past the guard towers and barbed wire and machine gun posts to an awaiting open-topped military car complete with twin Nazi flags on the front fenders and the German Cross on each door. Etienne Pasquier had his cello case, Akoka his clarinet, and Messiaen his haversack containing his treasured possessions. The clandestine affair seemed a dream. With permission from Kommandant Bielas, Hauptmann Brüll removed the musicians from Stalag 8A without any interference from anyone.

At the train station in Görlitz, Brüll accompanied the men down the depot's platform to the awaiting train.

"If the Gestapo ever discovers my indiscretion, I will be sent to a concentration camp with all the other disobedient German soldiers. Now hurry and catch that train and don't look back, especially you, Akoka. Imagine it: Germans releasing a Jew into freedom. They'd never believe it. Get going! *Macht schnell!*"

Just as the men were about to board the train, two German SS officers wearing the all too familiar swastika armbands approached them. Brüll motioned for the men to continue moving and board the train.

Several German soldiers accompanied the SS officers. The SS were in black and grey black uniforms; the double ancient Germanic Rune symbols of the *Souelu*, the insignia of the Schutzstaffel adorned their collar tabs.

Messiaen looked at his companions, dreading the worst of their fears. To have come so far: eluding death on the battlefield, surviving bombing raids, enduring the heat and dehydration of the temporary camp at Toul, and outlasting the cold and starvation of the Stalag, only to be detained by the SS moments from freedom.

Messiaen, Akoka, and Pasquier abruptly stopped. A plain-clothed Gestapo officer wearing a brown leather jacket demanded to see the men's papers. Messiaen went first and presented his documents.

"An orderly?" the Gestapo officer asked him.

"*Oui.*" Messiaen felt sweat forming on his forehead and trickling down his back.

The officer looked at the papers and then back at Messiaen. "Your hands are stained with ink."

"I am also a composer," Messiaen explained.

Messiaen was wearing a scarf that Brüll had given him.

"Where did you get this?" The German fingered the colorful scarf about Messiaen's neck.

"It was a gift."

"Go," he said, pushing Messiaen along.

Etienne Pasquier was let through without so much as a question as the Nazi glanced at his papers. Messiaen and Pasquier safely stepped on board the passenger car.

Henri Akoka followed by presenting his papers to the officer who looked at them and sent him forward as well. But just as Akoka was stepping up into the rail car, one of the SS officers on the train stopped him with a hand to the chest. "Halt! You step down."

"What? I am to be repatriated. All of my papers are in order. I am a *soldat-musicien.*"

Brüll was standing on the platform bewildered at what was happening.

"Detain him," the Gestapo officer ordered as two SS men swiftly took him into custody. "We have questions for you before you are returned to Stalag 8A."

"What? I am to be repatriated!" Akoka repeated, eyes wide with astonishment.

"*Nein, nein*, not you," the Gestapo officer laughed, as he revealed a cigarette and lit it.

"Why?" Brüll and Akoka asked simultaneously.

"*Jude.*" Jew. The Gestapo officer exhaled smoke in Akoka's face.

Akoka, the one man who had every legal right to be repatriated, was being stopped owing to his ethnic and religious background.

"Allow me to show you my foreskin," Henri Akoka acted as if he was about to pull down his pants. "I am uncircumcised." His circumcision had been performed poorly and he was able to escape detection in the past, passing as a gentile.

"You are under arrest." The SS guards took him inside the railway station.

As Henri was being escorted away he uttered in French, "*Un prisonnier, c'est fait pour s'évader,*" (a prisoner is made to escape).

"Remember the birds, Henri," Messiaen called out in French. "Remember the birds!" He wanted to say more, but the face of one of the SS officers was now inches from his own.

The remainder of Messiaen's thoughts remained unvoiced. *Fly, Henri. Fly like a bird!*

"You are Hauptmann Brüll, correct?" The Gestapo officer turned back to Brüll with the question.

"*Ja*," Brüll replied.

"These papers all seem to have been in proper order," the officer held his cigarette between his fingers. "Even Kommandant Bielas signed off."

"*Ja wohl.* Indeed. The man was—is——a *soldat-musicien*. The others were orderlies."

"Am I correct in my understanding that you are a half-Belgian Catholic who is a Jewish sympathizer?" He flicked away his half-smoked cigarette.

"I have never disobeyed an order, Sir."

The Gestapo officer laughed at him. "A German who loves Jews? What a disgrace to the uniform. Can you imagine any of your fellow Germans treating a Jew in this manner? How dare you regard him as your equal?!"

"He is a soldier, a patriot, and a musician," retorted Brüll.

The officer revealed his gun and pointed it at Brüll's chest, but put it away with a laugh. "Jew-lover! You've betrayed the Reich. You're coming with us," the Gestapo officer said. "We have some questions for you, Hauptmann Brüll."

Henri Akoka and Karl Albert Brüll were taken away, leaving Messiaen and Pasquier looking on in horror. *Brüll did so much for us,* thought Messiaen to himself. *Now the Good Samaritan is paying for his crime of decency. And this was to be Henri Akoka's last escape, but now he is one more sacrificial lamb led to slaughter.*

Messiaen held his haversack tightly, the contents of which had been his succor in his hunger and illness, the horrendous heat of summer, the deepest cold of winter, and the darkest hours of his captivity. In some ways his music had also comforted the German soldiers who, for good or ill, were beholden to serve Hitler's Reich. Now all of his hopes and prayers seemed to be unraveling for his Jewish friend, Akoka, and the German guardian and agent of mercy, Hauptmann Brüll.

Messiaen and Pasquier were powerless to do anything as the engineer tooted the engine's whistle and the train began to pull out of the station. Messiaen prayed for Akoka as well as Brüll, who had clearly violated Nazi dictates in securing their release.

If Hauptmann Brüll's forgeries of the documents were discovered, he could either be sent to the Russian front or be sent to one of the concentration camps or work camps for Jews and traitors to the Reich.

*****

Elated at his release yet mortified at Akoka and Brüll's arrest, Messiaen was numb. Though Messiaen was free, it was like a dream. He could scarcely believe it. He sighed as he watched the countryside go by the windows of the railway coach, so relieved that he was en route to freedom. Yet he still feared it was all too good to be true. After only a few kilometers, the rhythm of the train lulled Messiaen asleep.

When the two men arrived in Constance, Switzerland, they spent several days there in quarantine before being driven through France to Lyons where they awaited liberation from German custody.

The German Nazi officer in charge of the men resented having to release them to freedom and confronted Messiaen on the railway platform at Lyons. This German was a physical specimen of a man with bright blue eyes and near-perfect teeth, though prematurely bald. His black dress uniform with the red arm band revealing the swastika was meticulously cared for, and medals littered his chest, including the Iron Cross, while his pistol was strapped at his side.

"So. You are the French composer," the decorated Nazi spoke, avoiding eye contact at first. "Olivier Messiaen."

"*Oui.*"

"Professor Messiaen," he said with a pause, his malicious grin revealing his teeth, and his eyes now glaring at Messiaen. "Yes, I have heard your music..." His grin turned to a grimace. "It is objectionable. It belongs behind barbed wire along with the rest of the enemies of the Reich."

"It only sounds wretched to the untrained ear," Messiaen explained.

Pasquier gave Messiaen a disapproving look.

"Bravely spoken, Frenchie," he snorted. "What will you do with your freedom once you get back to Paris? France is the same as before; only better, more disciplined with Germany reigning over all."

"I am sure there are some who disagree," Messiaen replied calmly.

"But not you, correct?" He was breathing in Messiaen's face, his leather boots squeaking as he faced him.

Messiaen said nothing as his knees buckled. His eyes were fixed upon the twin lightning bolt emblems, the insignia of the Schutzstaffel on the officers' lapels.

"When we repatriate you, Professor Messiaen, you will collaborate and we will watch you closely. If you betray our trust, who knows what will happen to your wife or son?!" the man said quietly though forcefully. "We have ways of keeping order in Paris. In other words, you have no choice but to collaborate."

"You may intimidate me, but I will never embrace the Nazi reign. I am aware of your regime's methods. And I now return to *Occupied* France," he answered. "My beloved France."

Messiaen smiled sadly, not out of grief or anxiety, but a smile of resignation, knowing that nothing totally satisfied, not his work, not his knowledge. His sadness revealed a deeper joy that was ever elusive.

He realized that his music was not actually his own to possess but all was a gift, a gift of God and his fellow musicians. Indeed, the entire quartet was the result of the great crucible of the war in which he and his fellow musicians had been plunged, the cross of his wife's illness that he bore, his subsequent capture, his nearly dying, his imprisonment, and the constant threat of the SS.

But what if he hadn't ever gone to war? Would the quartet have ever been written, or at least written the way it was? Would he have ever created the music the way he did without being imprisoned? He'd like to think so. And even though the quartet received accolades and adulation, he still felt unsatisfied, unhappy, unfulfilled. He still yearned for something more.

Messiaen held his haversack on his way home bearing the knowledge that he had created something totally other: music without time. And that had he never been captured or imprisoned, the quartet may have likely never been written or even conceived.

*****

Chapter 23

Return

On 10 March 1941, Messiaen returned to Paris by train and could finally declare himself free again. Though he was living in the heart of occupied France, there were tears of joy in his eyes and songs on his lips.

He returned to his apartment in Paris and collected some clean clothes and obtained a pass to leave occupied France to travel to Neussargues in the Vichy free zone to be reunited with Claire and Pascal at the Delbos' family chateau.

Spring was in the air – the lovely sight of budding trees, the bright sunlight, fresh mountain air, rippling streams, the smell of rain, the flutter of wings, and sounds of singing birds brought back a surge of memories of he and Claire hiking the Cantal Mountains, enjoying nature, and spending time in the garden at Neussargues, her playing the violin, and he composing. The sweet melody of bird songs welcomed him home. He opened the iron gate of the brick wall that enclosed the chateau and walked the last few meters to the door.

On his first visit to the Delbos's chateau more than a decade before, Claire was watching from the upstairs window when she saw him enter the gate; she ran to meet him in the garden halfway between the front door and the gate.

Today was very different.

Standing before the great oaken door of the Delbos's home with his valise in his left hand, he rang the bell with his right. He heard footsteps approaching from inside. The door was unbolted and slowly opened revealing Madame Delbos.

"Madame Delbos," Messiaen nodded at his mother-in-law, seeing in her facial features those of his wife.

"Olivier," she exclaimed, embracing him, "Claire has longed for your return." Her face could not hide her shock at seeing the changes in his appearance. Messiaen was self-conscious of the fact that he had lost so much weight, his clothes hanging even more unevenly upon his sickly, lanky figure, and his hands and fingers swollen and disfigured.

"Where is Claire?" he asked plaintively, adjusting the eyeglasses on his face, straightening his sleeves at his wrists.

"Upstairs," Madame Delbos replied flatly. "Go to her."

"How is she?" Olivier asked, his eyes meeting his mother-in-law's.

"She is with Pascal," Madame Delbos answered, avoiding the question. "Pascal will be so happy to see his Papá back again."

Messiaen slowly but steadily walked the familiar hall, his feet creaking on the oak floorboards. He ascended the stairs slowly but steadily, preparing himself to meet his wife after their long separation.

Once he was at the top of the stairwell, he turned towards her room. His first glimpse of Claire was of her seated in a chair, a slightly slumped silhouette surrounded by light flooding the window frame. As he stepped into the room, Claire turned towards him and Pascal looked up. Her eyes spoke recognition, but the four-and-a-half-year-old's did not. Messiaen had known there would be that possibility, after more than a year and a half of being away, and especially given his compromised physical condition after his capture and imprisonment.

"Oli," Claire said, as she gazed upon him, her voice weak. "I dreamt that you were home, but it cannot be true." She seemed distant.

"Mi," he hurried to Claire, held her face between his hands, kissed her on both cheeks, then knelt at her feet, took her right hand from her lap, kissed it and held it to his chest. "Claire. I am here. I have returned."

"Pascal, say hello to your father," Claire said, this time a bit stronger as she reached for Pascal.

"Papá?" Pascal said as he walked to Messiaen.

"Son...my son," Messiaen said as Pascal looked suspiciously at this stranger. "My Pascal," Messiaen exclaimed as he knelt to cradle the child close.

"Is it really you?" Claire slowly stood and bent over, hugging Olivier and Pascal. "I feared...I feared...I feared you would be killed on your way home." Her embrace was empty of passion.

"It is I, my love," Olivier said, kissing her on the forehead and cheek. "I am alive."

"I had so many nightmares of you dying in battle, dying in the prison camp, dying at the hands of Nazi soldiers," Claire cried, pushing her hair from her eyes. "Oh, let me love you as from the beginning." He entered her embrace again.

The two walked downstairs and went to the garden with Pascal. It was clear that the war had not only taken its toll upon himself, but upon his beloved Claire and son Pascal.

"You are the love of my life, Claire." Messiaen said as he held her close, watching Pascal run towards his pedal car.

"How much longer before this war is over?" she asked, holding his right hand tightly in her left, steadying herself as she walked.

"I have no idea. I fear it is far from over." Silence reigned between them.

Together they recounted the past year and a half that they had been apart. Her appearance was not the same, nor was her mind, yet neither was his appearance the same, nor his sanity. There were circles under her eyes and her speech was altered, slightly slurred and erratic. She walked more slowly and her embrace seemed feeble.

That night he and Claire renewed their musical marriage: she played the violin as he accompanied her on the piano; they made love and spoke the words only lovers can understand. But things were different.

At breakfast the next morning, Claire admitted that her health was not good. "I am so confused at times," she said, weeping. "At times I forget how to read music. And simple words no longer come to mind easily."

"Oh, my little Mi," he leaned next to her and held her close. "I love you so. We will see the doctor." She still wanted to give him another child, but they both knew that her doctor had advised against her becoming pregnant again.

Her doctor in Neussargues could find nothing wrong, yet by the end of that first week, Olivier knew that his life with Claire would never be the same.

His memories of the war and his imprisonment became his nightmares. Eventually he left for Paris promising to arrange for Claire and Pascal's return to Paris.

On 13 April, Easter Sunday, Messiaen returned to Holy Trinity Church for Mass where he received a hero's welcome. He attempted to resume his life as a civilian.

*****

On 16 May 1941 Henri Akoka arrived in the French Free Zone and found Messiaen at his apartment.

"*Mon Dieu!*" Messiaen exclaimed at the sight of Akoka. "You're alive! You did it! You escaped!"

"Why did you ever doubt me?" Akoka laughed as the two men embraced. "Where is your faith in Man?"

"My indomitable Jewish Trotskyite!" Messiaen looked at him, still incredulous that Akoka was a free man, in the heart of occupied Paris.

He informed Messiaen that both he and Hauptmann Brüll had been released by the Gestapo and returned to Stalag 8A shortly after their detainment at the railway station in Gorlitz.

As for Henri Akoka, within a few days of being back at Stalag 8A, he was removed again, due to an order from the Geneva Convention calling for Algerians and African-born prisoners of war to be transported to warmer, milder climates. Akoka, due to his dark skin, Semitic features, and being Algerian-born, passed for an Arab, and in March 1941 he was transferred to Dinan, Brittany, in northwestern France. However, he was not liberated as promised. Within the month of April 1941 he, along with most of the other prisoners, was ordered back to Stalag 8A. Somehow, through everything, Akoka was still in possession of his clarinet.

The rumor was, however, that the prisoners were not being sent back to their original prisoner of war camps but were being sent to concentration camps. When the Germans loaded the prisoners back on cattle cars promising to return them to their respective prison camps, Akoka swore he was not going to be killed and took matters into his own hands.

As the cattle cars were loaded with the prisoners, the German guards designated one prisoner per car as chief. If anyone escaped, the chief would be shot. Henri Akoka volunteered to be chief of his car because he planned to escape and he didn't want any of the others to be shot.

"This Jewish Trotskyite won't be fooled again," Akoka told his fellow prisoners. "Those of us who are Jewish have heard the rumors of concentration camps and I am taking no chances. The damned Gestapo is looking for my brother Georges and my other brother is already a POW. My sister and mother have assumed false identities in order to escape the Gestapo. So, speaking for myself, I'm jumping off this crazy train!"

As the train passed through the French village of *Sainte-Julien-du-Sault*, Henri climbed through the roof of the rail car and in the dark of night, armed only with his clarinet, he jumped from the roof of the transport train as it rolled along at full speed.

Upon leaping from the train, Henri fell onto a riverbank and fainted from the shock of the fall, injuring his left hand. His clarinet was miraculously spared any damage. That morning, two railway switchmen discovered him lying unconscious and brought him to a French doctor to bandage his wounds. The switchmen made the doctor promise to contact the German authorities. The doctor promised to do so.

When the switchmen left, the doctor treated Akoka for his injuries. Henri pleaded with the doctor not to contact the Germans.

"Have no fear," the doctor smiled as he bandaged Akoka's left hand. "I have no such intention of doing anything of the kind."

Henri was speechless as the doctor smiled at him. "I'm not going to turn you in," the doctor explained. "I am, however, going to hide you."

So the French physician hid Henri Akoka in his home for over a month and restored him to health by feeding him, treating his shrapnel wounds, and healing his injuries from the jump from the train. At great personal risk, the doctor even drove him to the Free Zone; a French Catholic risking his own life for a Jew he didn't even know.

Akoka's unconquerable spirit enabled him to secure a clarinet post in the *Orchestre National de la Radio*, in the Free Zone of Marseilles where he resumed his orchestra job.

*****

In May, Messiaen began teaching harmony at the Paris Conservatoire. The students were shocked at the sight of Messiaen's chilblains on account of the privations which he had suffered during his time in captivity in Silesia, and they were surprised that he could still play the piano with such deformed hands, for Messiaen was very thin and his hands and fingers were still swollen.

By Christmas 1941, Claire and Pascal returned to Paris. Messiaen took Claire to a doctor there in an attempt to diagnose her illness. As he waited in the doctor's office for Claire to emerge from her appointment, he meditated upon the beads of his rosary. The smell of iodine and antiseptic and sight of medical paraphernalia preoccupied his mind.

Finally, the doctor came out to Messiaen and explained Claire's illness as best he could. "Claire is ill and will likely never recover. It seems to be some kind of early dementia or mental disorder. There is a possibility that she has suffered from a stroke sometime in the past."

Messiaen felt as if he was going to pass out. He dropped into a chair in the waiting room and clutched his satchel full of musical scores. After the doctor departed, Claire emerged from the examination room and embraced Messiaen. Messiaen kept his emotions in check as he left the hospital with her arm in his. Two turtle doves on the steps took flight as Olivier and Claire approached. The doves' wings whistled as they flew away. Messiaen couldn't help but think that he and Claire were once like the pair of doves, soaring high above the earth in rapture. Though Claire could no longer fly as she did before, he would remain faithful to her, just as God had been faithful to him during the war and his imprisonment.

Regardless of the diagnosis of Claire's illness, it was a tragic martyrdom. Claire was Olivier Messiaen's light and inspiration, his friend, colleague, and fellow composer. But now she was a mere shell of the woman he once knew and loved. The love of Claire was physically spent and the grim winter of her illness robbed Olivier Messiaen of the summertime of his marriage.

Claire began to decline invitations to dinner and became restless and let things fall apart around her, neglecting housework, even becoming forgetful of her personal appearance and hygiene. Messiaen returned to his routine of composing and performing, nearly obsessed with his passion for music. As Claire's health continually declined, her mother and sister came to Paris to help care for her and Pascal in 1942.

In the face of Claire's fate, Messiaen was haunted by the memory of his own mother's great sadness and premature death. The pain was so deep that he felt as if he was sharing in Claire's illness. His work became his escape, his way of dealing with the pain and heartbreak.

He found the whole unfolding tragedy of her illness to be more severe than the war. In the camp, he was surrounded by a community of men who were all suffering a common fate, but with Claire he suffered alone.

Claire had been a tremendous part of his life before he was called up for duty and subsequently imprisoned. Now, overcome by the reality of losing the love of his life, he had become a dove who had lost his mate and flew away into the realm of his music and prayer.

The myth of a love that could only be consummated fully in death was now to be his life. Despite all this, Messiaen remained true to Claire, honoring his marriage vows, all the while mourning her as he watched her health and mind decline as she slipped into another world. She was no longer the poised virtuoso, the beautiful violinist with whom he had fallen in love. She had become a mournful dove with a broken wing, a joyless nightingale who could no longer sing.

*****

Epilogue

As for Jean Le Boulaire, he and two other prisoners escaped Stalag 8A in October of 1941; however, they were recaptured three days later and returned to solitary confinement. Then in December of 1941, Hauptmann Brüll aided Jean Le Boulaire in the same manner that he had helped Messiaen and Pasquier: by forging Jean Le Boulaire's repatriation papers, thereby securing his release to France.

Jean Le Boulaire changed his name to Jean Lanier after the war and became an actor, starring in such films as *The Soft Skin,* directed by François Truffaut. Ironically, Jean never played the violin professionally again, though he is largely remembered as the violinist who had debuted Messiaen's *Quartet for the End of Time.* He died in 1999.

*****

Henri Akoka, after his narrow escape from the Nazi roundups, returned to civilian life as a clarinetist. However, anti-Semitic fervor was taking hold in parts of France. The Vichy government required all Jews in the Occupied Zone to register. This included Henri's father and mother. Members of the French Resistance were also being pursued by the Pro-German Vichy government.

On 13 December 1941, the French police arrested Henri Akoka's father, Abraham, in the middle of the night. He was arrested not because he was Jewish, but because his fourth son, Georges, was active in the French Resistance. Unable to find Georges, the French police arrested Abraham in his place. The French police turned him over to the German authorities and his whereabouts were never disclosed. He was never heard from again. After the war, the Akoka family learned that Abraham had been sent to Auschwitz where he was put to death shortly after arriving there.

Henri Akoka died in 1975.

*****

Etienne Pasquier and his brothers Jean (violinst) and Pierre (Violist) resumed their performances as the Pasquier Trio. Etienne died in 1997.

*****

Hauptmann Karl-Albert Brüll returned to civilian life after war resuming his practice of law in Görlitz, in newly established East Germany. Following a failed insurrection in 1948 against the Communist government, Brüll was condemned to three years of forced labor. After his liberation, he went to work for the West German government.

He and Olivier Messiaen never met again, though Messiaen did send him a note thanking him for his assistance in securing his release from Stalag 8A. Brüll once visited Paris and rang Messiaen, but for some reason Messiaen declined the opportunity to see him.

*****

In late March and April 1941, Olivier Messiaen spent six weeks in Vichy, France. Though Messiaen's sentiments were likely not with the Vichy Government, "before returning to Paris in April 1941, Messiaen wrote two choruses for *Portique pour une fille de France*, a celebration of Joan of Arc commissioned by the Vichy government. Plenty of artists strongly involved in the French Resistance wrote works to government commission, and worked in government-funded institutions during the occupation (Poulenc and Desormière to name but two very prominent resistance members). Messiaen really had very little political sensibility at all – like the vast majority of people in occupied France, who neither embraced the Nazi regime, nor felt able to resist in an active manner; he was primarily concerned with the basics of putting food on the table. He was neither saint nor sinner during the occupation, but just wanted it to end."[1]

Oliver Messiaen was appointed Professor of Harmony at the Paris Conservatoire after his release from Stalag 8A in 1941, and became

---

[1] Christopher Dingle, e-mail correspondence, 12 May 2010.

professor of composition there in 1966. Christopher Dingle writes, concerning the letter of 21 August 1940, "The mention of Messiaen's post at the Paris Conservatoire is a little puzzling since, so far as we know, Messiaen did not begin working there until *after* the war. It is possible that there had been moves, possibly by Marcel Dupré, to appoint him in 1939, but that these were interrupted by the outbreak of war. Messiaen was a music professor at the *Ecole Normale* at the outbreak of the war."[2]

Messiaen held both positions until he retired in 1978. Among his many pupils were Pierre Boulez, notable in his own right, and Yvonne Loriod, who, after Claire died in 1959, married Messiaen in 1961. Yvonne Loriad was likely the most important interpreter of Messiaen's piano works and, beginning in the 1940s, she premiered most of Messiaen's works for the piano. Messiaen was well known for his devout Roman Catholic religious beliefs and his love of nature. As a passionate ornithologist, he spent much of his time transforming bird songs into musical notation and many of his compositions during the rest of his life drew upon these transcriptions. Messiaen died 28 April 1992. Yvonne Loriad Messiaen died 17 May 2010.

*****

Claire Delbos Messiaen's health issues were likely the result of a combination of factors: depression over her miscarriages; hereditary predisposition to blood clotting during pregnancy; deprivation of oxygen during childbirth; post-partum depression after birth; and Olivier being sent off to war, leaving her alone with a toddler.

Any type of surgery could lead to hypoxic or anoxic brain injury, depending on the skill of the anesthesiologist and the underlying health of the patient.

A history of miscarriages can also indicate an underlying hereditary hypercoagulable state (predisposition to blood clots) which could lead to stroke and cognitive problems. Inherited clotting disorders have been implicated in both miscarriage and strokes.

[2] Ibid.

Antiphospholipid antibody syndrome is characterized by recurrent spontaneous miscarriage in women, blood clots (which may manifest as heart attack, stroke, or even a series of microvascular brain infarcts, or "mini-strokes," which may resemble atherosclerotic dementia, occurs in younger women), and thrombocytopenia (low platelet count, where "clotting packets" in the blood clump together).

Antiphospholipid antibody syndrome may occur as a distinct diagnosis, or it may be seen in context of a patient with systemic lupus erythematosus, an autoimmune disorder that typically affects women of child-bearing age.

By the end of the war, her memory loss and mental disorder had worsened. In 1945 she had a hysterectomy and the surgery only seemed to make her mental condition worse. Some medication that she received might have contained heavy metals such as mercury, cadmium, or arsenic that could have contributed to memory loss or some form of psychosis. Even a lack of oxygen at any point during the birthing procedure and/or her subsequent hysterectomy could have also contributed to her progressive memory loss and cognitive problems.

By the early 1950s, she didn't even recognize a violin, let alone know what it was for. Finally, Messiaen had to place her in a sanatorium where she remained institutionalized, with increasingly failing health. Claire died in 1959.

*****

As for Pascal Messiaen, life was difficult for him after his mother's death, and as a teenager he and his father were distant – mostly because of Olivier Messiaen's preoccupation with composing and performing which consumed his days and nights. Olivier did not attend his son's wedding, although by the time Claire had died, he and his son were reconciled.

"It would be the highest compliment
to me as a composer
if you had a spiritual experience
because of hearing my music."

- Olivier Messiaen

Olivier Messiaen

Final Notes

"The first performance of the *Quartet for the End of Time* at the Stalag in January 1941 has, together with the premiere of *The Rite of Spring*, become one of the great stories of twentieth-century music," wrote Paul Griffiths in his 1985 book, *Olivier Messiaen and the Music of Time*. I agree wholeheartedly, thus the genesis of this book.

Michael R. Linton writes: "Messiaen told *The New York Times* that while the sole purpose of his music was to point people to Christ, somehow even his greatest enthusiasts usually seemed blind to his intent. They admired and even praised his work, but cared little – or purposefully ignored – its message. This failure, or refusal, of so many musicians to understand his music was the greatest sorrow of Messiaen's artistic life. But the miracle of the *Quatour* – perhaps the greatest artistic miracle of our times – remains."[3]

"Certainly, there are many reasons that Messiaen thought fit to compose a piece for the end of time," Sudeep Agawala writes. "Messiaen's musical narrative takes place at the end of a social and political era—World War II was ushering in a world of economic hardship for the national leaders of the free world; Nazi persecution, torture, and mass murders were re-defining the image of humanity and the regard for human life in terrifying new ways; scientific developments magnified human power over nature to previously unthinkable levels and revolutionized its perception of reality. The ways in which the old regimes were changing were not necessarily exciting or hopeful. In fact, many of the recent developments seemed the opposite. However, written in a German war camp, about the end of the world, the end of time, Messiaen's piece, steely in its portrayal of God and the Apocalypse still manages optimism. Messiaen's end is not one of fire, inhumanity and mass destruction. His world saw the end in praise of eternal comfort and glory."

---

[3] *First Things*: 87 (November 1998) 13-15.

Messiaen was once asked: "Does a listener have to have had a spiritual experience to appreciate your music?" "Not at all," he replied, "but it would be the highest compliment to me as a composer if you had a spiritual experience because of hearing my music."

As a prisoner-composer, Messiaen witnessed to the kingdom of Christ. As the Christian is called to be *in* the world, but not *of* the world, so Messiaen was *in* time but not *of* Time.

The three musicians and Messiaen represent the social, religious, philosophical, and political viewpoints of their contemporaries of the early 20th century. Nonetheless, these four very different men collaborated as a harmonious quartet to create musical history in the most unlikely of places. The *Quartet for the End of Time* is hailed as one of the most sublime pieces of chamber music composed in the 20th Century.

"There is no doubt that time stood still while these four prisoners played," Graham Pellettieri wrote, "bringing warmth and light to so many who desperately needed it, during one of the coldest and darkest times in human history. The uncertainty of both the prison environment and the outcome of the war created a 'timeless' effect for the prisoners."

"By 1941, this composer [Messiaen] no longer wanted to hear time being beaten out by a drum—*one, two, three, four;* he had had enough of that in the war," writes Alex Ross, music critic for *The New Yorker.* "Instead, he devised rhythms that expanded, contracted, stopped in their tracks, and rolled back in symmetrical patterns…This is the music of one who expects paradise not only in a single awesome hereafter but also in the happenstance epiphanies of daily life. In the face of hate, this honestly Christian man did not ask, 'Why, O Lord?' He said, 'I love you'."

Throughout his imprisonment, Messiaen suffered numerous hardships, including starvation, freezing temperatures, and chilblains, but he stayed true to his interests in poetry, birds, and Catholicism. His religious faith included a fascination with mysticism and the supernatural.

Messiaen had a love for the scripture, especially the Book of the Apocalypse, *The Revelation of St. John,* with its description of the end of Time. It foretells that Christ's death and resurrection would ultimately redeem the world.

"I have not written liturgical music but rather meditative music on the mysteries of faith," he said. "These works can be played in church, or in concert, or in the open air. I want to write music that is an act of faith, a music that is about everything without ceasing to be about God."

Maurice Emmanuel, composer and historian wrote: "In an environment where faith plays little part, he [Messiaen] has commanded admiration and respect through the dignity of his lifestyle and the genuinely Christian warmth of his personality."

Messiaen was the caged bird who sang despite his captivity. He longed for freedom and his faith in the unseen filled him with hope.

In the words of Messiaen scholar, Rebecca Rischin: "The Quartet stands as Messiaen's triumph over time. On 15 January 1941, Messiaen realized his dream of the bird. Where all around him men were making war, Messiaen, like a bird, was making music."

To the avant-garde, he was too traditional and too religious; to the traditionalists and religious, he was too avant-garde. As a result he will always stand somewhere outside of Time. In the words of Messiaen: Eternity is not a long period of time; it is no time at all.

As a small child I recall once asking my father why people sang. His immediate response was: "Because of Easter." At the time the answer was more cryptic than helpful, but I have never forgotten his answer. My father neither recalls my question nor his response, but in retrospect he believes that it was a rather profound response for one untrained in theology. Whether my father knew it or not, he echoed the sentiments of Olivier Messiaen; for without the Resurrection of Christ the Christian is bereft of hope.

Music was always a part of my life as I grew up; from my parents playing the radio to the good Sisters of Providence getting us to sing every morning at Mass. Yet I can attribute my initial interest in classical music to Dr. Bernard Verkamp, philosophy professor at Vincennes University, who gave me a complimentary ticket to a performance by the Indiana University Music Department at Vincennes on the occasion of Johann Sebastian Bach's 300th birthday, March 25, 1985. I am forever indebted to Dr. Verkamp's insight into encouraging me to attend the concert. Bach's music opened a door to another world for me and Bach and all "his musical children," in the words of Mozart, have been constant companions ever since.

Father Columba Kelly, O.S.B., of Saint Meinrad Archabbey, a Gregorian Chant scholar and musicologist, then deepened my love for music while I was a student in his Music Appreciation class at Saint Meinrad in 1986.

Ever since my youth, however, I have had a love for the pipe organ. It all began with hearing our church organist playing the works of J.S. Bach, Charles-Marie Widor, César Franck, Marcel Dupré, and Maurice Duruflé on the pipe organ at the Old Cathedral in Vincennes, Indiana. Over the years the works of Francis Poulenc, Felix Alexandre Guilmant, Josef Rheinberger, John Tavener and John Rutter have enriched my life.

From hearing the pipe organ at the Old Cathedral in Vincennes, Indiana, Saint Meinrad, Indiana, Our Lady of Hope in Washington, Indiana, and other places such as the Basilica of the Immaculate Conception in Washington, D.C., Westminster Cathedral in London, England, Notre Dame in Paris, France, and the Basilica of Santa Maria del Fiore (the Duomo) in Florence, or from listening to *Pipe Dreams* on Public Radio, my love for the instrument has not diminished.

In January 2009 while searching for organ works at the downtown Evansville library, I came across a collection of organ works by Olivier Messiaen. I had heard a piece by him in the past, but I really didn't know much about him. Immediately upon listening to his *Apparition de l'église éternelle*, Vision of the Eternal Church, I knew I had met a kindred spirit.

Messiaen said, "What comes from the organ is invisible music, propelled by wind, yet whose instrument gives no sign of activity, and whose player normally cannot be seen. Organ music symbolizes and makes real the contact between the mundane and the eternal. Indeed it makes a sacrament of all the world." I concur.

I then began to explore more of his musical world and soon discovered that he truly spoke to my soul: He loved birds, he was a Catholic, and he loved the pipe organ. I soon obtained an audio copy of the *Quatuor pour la Fin du Temps* and learned of the unique story behind its composition. I soon began collecting his works and found myself returning to them often, meditating upon them, listening to them over and over again.

In April of 2009, my wife and I attended an organ recital at Saint Meinrad Archabbey where the organist played Olivier Messiaen's *L'Ascension*. Due to the warm spring weather, the monks had opened the windows of the church. As Messiaen's work was played I could not help but note the chirping of birds, sparrows, crows, a mockingbird, but in particular there was a blue jay that must have been perched on one of the windowsills. His call and chirps were quite noticeable. And I wondered if perhaps Olivier Messiaen was smiling upon us, for he loved birdsongs very much. I took it as a sign and it was then that I decided to write his story. Providentially, my wife and I sat next to Father Columba Kelly, O.S.B. at this very recital and afterwards he gave us an impromptu exposition on the piece.

It was shortly thereafter that I discovered Rebecca Rischin's work *For the End of Time: The Story of the Messiaen Quartet*. Her work confirmed my decision to write the story in novel form. I am indebted to her research and insights into the life of Messiaen, and all the other individuals whose contributions allowed the *The Miracle of Stalag 8A* to become a reality. In many ways I feel as if I went off to war and was imprisoned in Stalag 8A with Olivier Messiaen.

When Messiaen read the Book of the Apocalypse, or Revelation, he was intrigued by the tenth chapter:

> *And I saw another mighty angel come down from heaven, clothed with a cloud: and a rainbow was upon his head, and his face was as it were the sun, and his feet as pillars of fire. In his hand he held a small scroll that had been opened. He then set his right foot upon the sea, and his left foot on the land....*
>
> *Then the angel I saw standing on the sea and on the land raised his right hand to heaven and swore by the one who lives forever and ever, who created heaven and earth and sea and all that is in them, "There shall be no more Time, but on the day of the*

seventh Angel's trumpet the mystery of God shall be accomplished."

The angel mentioned so often by Messiaen held a scroll. The scripture passage continues:

> *Then the voice that I had heard from heaven spoke to me again and said, "Go, take the scroll that lies open in the hand of the angel who is standing on the sea and on the land." So I went up to the angel and told him to give me the small scroll. He said to me, "Take and swallow it. It will turn your stomach sour, but in your mouth it will taste as sweet as honey."*

> *I took the small scroll from the angel's hand and swallowed it. In my mouth it was like sweet honey, but when I had eaten it, my stomach turned sour. Then someone said to me, "You must prophesy again about many peoples, nations, tongues, and kings"* Rev. 10.8-11).

Ezekiel 3.1-4 reads similarly:

> *"Son of man, eat what is before you; eat this scroll, then go, speak to the house of Israel." So I opened my mouth and he gave me the scroll to eat. "Son of man," he then said to me, "feed your belly and fill your stomach with this scroll I am giving you." I ate it, and it was as sweet as honey in my mouth. He said: "Son of man, go now to the house of Israel, and speak my words to them."*

The art of *lectio divina* is usually applied to the practice of prayerfully reading scripture. There is no doubt that Olivier Messiaen practiced the art of *lectio* not only on scripture but on all of nature itself. In his musical legacy one can also find oneself in the presence of God by meditating upon his music.

When the person prayerfully reads scripture, one metaphorically consumes and digests the Word. Internalizing the Word in such depth allows it to become part of one's essence, one's soul, as its living and active presence is lived out in daily life. When one chants the scripture, God sings through him or her, rather than simply singing *to* God or only singing *about* God.

After the angel announces that there shall be no more time, the angel then instructs the hearer to eat the scroll, to allow the words to sink into his being. As Jeremiah the prophet proclaimed:

> *When I found your words, O Lord, I devoured them;*
> *They became my joy and the happiness of my heart*
> (Jer. 15.16).

As the believer sacramentally consumes the Body of Christ in order to become Christ to others, by allowing Christ to consume him or her, I believe Messiaen intended for the listener of his music to transcend time and be transported into, indeed find himself in, the presence of God. Therefore Messiaen was allowing the ineffable mystery of God to use his musical genius all for the glory and honor of God.

In many ways Messiaen will always stand somewhere outside of Time. His own words confirm this: *Eternity is not a long period of time; it is no time at all.*

It is my prayer that just as St. John took the sacred scroll from the angel and consumed the Word, the reader will partake of this incredible story and the music of Messiaen and be conveyed into the eternal presence of God.

John William McMullen
11 July 2010
Feast of Saint Benedict

Acknowledgments

The theologian John of Salisbury wrote: "We are like dwarfs sitting on the shoulders of giants. We see more, and things that are more distant, than they did, not because our sight is superior or because we are taller than they, but because they raise us up, and by their great stature add to ours."

At the end of writing this novel based upon the life and work of Olivier Messiaen, I admit I am standing on the shoulders of giants, such as Christopher Dingle, Nigel Simeone, Peter Hill, Paul Griffiths, Rebecca Rischin, Alex Ross, and many others who either knew the man Olivier Messiaen or those who have made it their business to know and understand his life and achievements. And no less thanks goes to the three men who made the quartet possible, Etienne Pasquier, Henri Akoka, and Jean Le Boulaire, and Messiaen's widow, Yvonne Loriad Messiaen, who promoted her husband's work her whole life.

Uniquely, I wish to thank Rebecca Rischin for her book, *FOR THE END OF TIME: THE STORY OF THE MESSIAEN QUARTET* (Cornell University Press, 2003; 2006), the definitive work on the Quartet for the End of Time, which helped to inspire this novel. Without her invaluable contribution and research on the Quartet for the End of Time, this book would have remained a pipe dream. To her and all of those whose work contributed to my own miracle, I thank you.

A special thank you is also in order for Katie Meyer, contributing editor *par excellence*, and Dr. Christopher Dingle, noted Messiaen scholar, for his editorial suggestions on the manuscript, and his contribution to the history of the life and music of Messiaen.

In gratitude to my readers and reviewers: Stephen Rode, Mike Whicker, and Dave Wathen for their contributions concerning the warfare and political minutiae of the World War II era; Father Harry Hagan, O.S.B., of Saint Meinrad Archabbey, for his knowledge of Gregorian chant and Liturgical history; Dr. Phillip Pierpont, former Academic Dean of Vincennes University and English Professor; Dr.

Eric Von Fuhrmann; Dr. Steven Scheer; Alfred Savia, Music Director and Conductor of the Evansville Philharmonic Orchestra; Glenn Roberts, Executive Director of the Evansville Philharmonic Orchestra; Kent Nagano, Conductor of the Montreal Symphony; and Joshua Bell, renowned Indiana violinist.

Also a special recognition is in order for former prisoner of war Guy Stevens of Boonville, Indiana, for sharing his firsthand experience of World War II, his capture, and living as a POW until being liberated by allied forces in 1945.

Thanks to Dr. Andy Hart, medical student Todd Wannemuehler, Pharmacist Christopher McMullen, and Dr. Richard Bell for their assistance in helping to diagnose some possible explanations for Claire Delbos Messiaen's mental and physical health problems.

Thanks to Larry Ordner, Indiana Senator Richard Lugar's Southwestern Indiana Regional Director, who was also an integral part of the *Veterans History Project*, which served to record stories of the lives and experiences of veterans and prisoners of war.

Finally, an incalculable thank you to my wife, Mary Grace: the miracle in my life, who has continually supported her husband with his dream of writing, and enduring over a year and a half of hearing nothing but Messiaen's music. And to my two sons, Andrew and Theodore, who allowed their father to go to war and be imprisoned in Stalag 8A with Olivier Messiaen.

Notes and Sources

Notes on Etienne Pasquier and Henri Akoka obtained from Rischin, Rebecca, *For the End of Time: The Story of the Messiaen Quartet*: (Cornell University Press, 2003; 2006), pages 9, 11, and 96.

Notes on Messiaen's arrival at Stalag 8A, Rischin, p. 22. Some of the information about the camp was obtained from Rischin, pps. 22-23.

Information on the monthly newspaper *Le Lumignon* found in Rischin page 25.

Some of the details concerning Jean Le Boulaire were obtained from Rischin, pps. 15 and 32.

Notes on Messiaen's fear of forgetting how to compose found in Rischin, p. 44.

Information about Bielas and Brüll's help in obtaining a cello for Pasquier found in Rischin, p. 34.

Information about Akoka's father gleaned from an interview by Rischin, p. 114; information of Akoka's escape and recapture found in Rischin, pps. 45-46.

Information concerning Messiaen being sought out for various reasons found in Rischin, p. 37.

Information on the camp stage, weather conditions, and Brüll's treatment of the men found in Rischin, pps. 34-35, 37-38.

Information concerning Jean Le Boulaire's childhood and war experience found in Rischin, p. 32; information about Jean Le Boulaire's views on Messiaen obtained from Rischin, pps. 40-43; information on Jean Le Boulaire, from Rischin p. 86; and Le Boulaire's loving memory of performing the last movement of the Quartet found in Ricschin p. 109-110.

Information concerning the sixth movement of The Quartet found in Rischin, pps. 52-54.

Information concerning the composition of the Quartet found in multiple sources, namely those mentioned on the bibliography page.

Messiaen's comment that his faith made him free found in Rischin, p. 51; his comment that the birds are greatest musicians and represent our longings, found in Rischin, pps 57 and 60.

Messiaen's descriptions of each movement is readily available and commonly known in the musical world, however, I relied upon Anthony Pople and Rebecca Rischin's translations.

Information regarding Brüll informing Messiaen that he and the other musicians may be released and the subsequent authorization by Bielas allowing Brüll to drive the Messiaen, Pasquier, and Akoka to the train station found in Rischin, p. 71-72.

Though Messiaen's sentiments may not have been with the Vichy Government, regarding Rischin's claim that Messiaen did not receive a commission from the Vichy Government (Rischin, p. 90), Messiaen scholar Dr. Christopher Dingle points to the fact that "before returning to Paris in April 1941, Messiaen wrote two choruses for *Portique pour une fille de France*, a celebration of Joan of Arc commissioned by the Vichy government. Plenty of artists strongly involved in the French Resistance wrote works to government commission, and worked in government-funded institutions during the occupation (Poulenc and Desormière, to name but two very prominent resistance members)." Christopher Dingle, e-mail correspondence, 12 May 2010.

Information concerning Henri Akoka and is father's fate found in Rischin, pps. 75, 77-78, 83-85. The Akoka family never knew what became of their father, Abraham, until after the war when it was discovered that Abraham Akoka had been sent to Auschwitz. He arrived on 23 September 1942 and was promptly gassed to death.

Bibliography

Bryant, Jen. Music for the end of time. (Illustrated by Beth Peck). Grand Rapids, Mich.: Eerdmans Books for Young Readers, 2005

Dingle, Christopher. The life of Messiaen. Cambridge, [England] : Cambridge University Press, 2007.

Hill, Peter and Nigel Simeone. Messiaen. New Haven, Conn.: Yale University Press, 2005.

Music for the End of Time by *Michael R. Linton*. First Things, 87 (November 1998) 13-15.

Pople, Anthony. Messiaen: *Quator pour la Fin du Temps*. Cambridge, UK: Camridge University Press, 1998.

Rischin, Rebecca, For the End of Time: The Story of the Messiaen Quartet. Ithaca, N.Y. (Cornell University Press, 2003; 2006).

Ross, Alex. Revelations: *The story behind Messiaen's "Quartet for the End of Time." The New Yorker* Magazine, March 22, 2004.

OLIVIER MESSIAEN
(1908 – 1992)

Quatuor pour la Fin du Temps (Quartet for the End of Time)

I. *Liturgie de cristal* [Crystal Liturgy]

II. *Vocalise pour l'ange qui annonce la Fin du Temps*
[Vocalise for the Angel who announces the End of Time]

III. *Abîme des oiseaux* [Abyss of the Birds]

IV. *Intermède* [Interlude]

V. *Louange à l'éternité de Jésus*
[Praise to the Eternity of Jesus]

VI. *Danse de la fureur, pour les sept trompettes*
[Dance of Fury, for the seven trumpets]

VII. *Fouillis d'arcs-en-ciel, pour l'ange qui annonce la Fin du Temps*
[Cluster of rainbows, for the Angel who announces the End of Time]

VIII. *Louange à immortalité de Jésus*
[Praise to the Immortality of Jesus]

John William McMullen has written and taught for over twenty years. He is the author of several books: *The Last Blackrobe of Indiana and the Potawatomi Trail of Death*; *Roman*; *Poor Souls*; and *Eugene & the Haunted Train Bridge*. He holds a Master's Degree in Theological Studies from Saint Meinrad School of Theology. He is a Philosophy Professor, Theologian, Permanent Deacon, and Historian. McMullen resides in Evansville, Indiana, with his wife and children.

Contact the author at: <u>johnmcmullen@insightbb.com</u>

Bird Brain Publishing

Bird Brain Publishing
Evansville, Indiana

To Delight, Instruct, and Inspire

Also from Bird Brain Publishing

The Last Blackrobe of Indiana and the Potawatomi Trail of Death

From the forgotten history of 1830s Indiana, John William McMullen unearths the true story of Benjamin Petit, a French Attorney turned missionary priest, and his mission to the Potawatomi People in the Diocese of Vincennes, Indiana. Under the urging of the saintly Bishop Simon Bruté, Petit joined the northern Indiana Potawatomi tribes in 1837, a year before their forced removal west. McMullen retells the incredible journey of Petit who traveled with the Potawatomi People and became part of their history.

"The deportation of Chief Menominee and his tribe of Potawatomi Indians from their reservation at Twin Lakes in Marshall County, in September, 1838, is one of the darkest pages in the history of Indiana. The farther in time we get away from this event the clearer this will appear and the more interest will be attached to the route which is consecrated by the blood of that helpless people at the hands of a civilized and Christian state: The Potawatomi Trail.

"Of all the names connected with this crime, there is one, Father Benjamin Petit, the Christian martyr, which stands like a star in the firmament, growing brighter and it will shine on through for ages to come." – Benjamin Stuart, Indiana journalist, early 20th century

POOR SOULS

JOHN WILLIAM McMULLEN

Praise for
POOR SOULS

"...The intention of this writer is to highlight the ordinary, and indeed the sinful, as being transformed by grace into something worthy of God. *Poor Souls* is a front-runner of the Catholic novel, though this is not immediately apparent because of its unpretentiousness.

"So why does it haunt me and why do I want to hail it as an outstanding Catholic novel? Because the writer is an unswervingly honest professional with something pertinent to say, and because he says it with quiet sobriety without ever resorting to 'pious-speak'."
– Leo Madigan, Fatima-Ophel Books

"POOR SOULS gives the reader a rollicking tale of seminarians and priests in their service of the church. McMullen, writing as an insider, masterfully strikes insightful chords of humor without resorting to ridicule." – Clark Gabriel Field, (The Celibate)

"An unexpected revelation of life in the seminary and parish, McMullen reveals the very human lives of Roman Catholic clergy knowingly yet lovingly. McMullen's novel is so real it will make you laugh and cry at the same time. Uproariously shrewd and marvelously told."
– Doug Chambers, (Earthrise)

ODD NUMBERS
by
M. Grace Bernardin

Is it possible to find love in the heart of the Midwest between a strip mall and a cornfield? This is the quest of three friends who meet in the 1980s at the Camelot Apartments, located amidst the suburban sprawl of the southern Indiana town of Lamasco.

Frank, who moves from the East coast to Lamasco to start a market research firm, is a well-bred, charming, polished Ivy Leaguer with a penchant for classical music.

Vicky, the noisy downstairs neighbor who is constantly trying to drown out Frank's classical music with rock and roll, is a tough-talking, whisky-guzzling, Harley-riding lady bartender from western Kentucky with a reckless spirit and a haunted past.

Between Frank and Vicky is Allison, an image-conscious, self-improvement junkie who gives up a promising marketing career in Chicago to return to her hometown of Lamasco at the urging of her high school sweetheart and fiancé, with whom she has long since fallen out of love.

An unlikely friendship forms between Allison and Vicky as they discover that underneath their very different veneers, they have many similarities, one of those being a secret passion for their neighbor, Frank.

ODD NUMBERS spans twenty-plus years and ultimately culminates with the startling collision that reconnects this odd love triangle.

Advance Praise for ODD NUMBERS

"Touching, clever, and at times delightfully off the wall, Odd Numbers is a gulp of fresh air. The best storytellers know that characters are everything, and Bernardin's characters Vicky, Allison, and Frank, are like us-flawed but hopeful.

"Bernardin's prose reminds me of Willa Cather, her descriptions elegant but not blustery or garish. Those among us who esteem a well-crafted sentence have a new wordsmith to add to our list of favorite writers. Odd Numbers is a finely crafted story of the human heart."

- Mike Whicker, author of the bestseller, *Invitation to Valhalla* and *Blood of the Reich* (Walküre Press)

"An inspiring read, courageously honest and full of hope for all of the flawed.... Deeply thoughtful characters revealing inner virtues and vices, outward strengths and weaknesses, climaxing in a sublime symphony of charity."

- Judy Lyden, author of *PORK CHOPS*

Bird Brain Publishing
Evansville, Indiana

To Delight, Instruct, and Inspire

www.birdbrainpublishing.com

LaVergne, TN USA
28 January 2011
214408LV00006B/62/P